Brave Little Girl

Emersyn Kane

Steadfast Publishing
U.S.A.

ACKNOWLEDGMENTS

There are so many people who have influenced my life and I didn't realize that until I wrote this book. While there are far too many to name, I would like to acknowledge those whose influence was, in my opinion, pivotal to who I have become. Not all assisted or supported me during the process of writing this book. However, they each had such a profound effect on my journey, that I believe I could not have arrived at the completion of this book without them.

First and foremost, I would like to acknowledge my parents. If you had been the parents, I wanted you to be, I wouldn't be the woman I am proud to be today. I blame you for making me strong; I blame you for making me courageous; I blame you for making me independent; I blame you for making me kind; and I blame you for making me love.

My sister; my rock; the one true consistency in my life. Your unwavering support and encouragement have allowed me to grow into the person I am today. You have believed in me and this book from the beginning and have remained absent of judgment and expectation. No words can express the gratitude I have for you.

My three beautiful children. The most amazing

accomplishments of my life. You have watched Mom do some hard work and fight the hard fight. I'm sure you have sacrificed and for that, I can only say thank you. Never will I turn away; no matter how gray the waters become. The three of you will forever be loved, accepted, and encouraged to live your lives. No regrets.

My loving, patient, supportive husband. You have walked this journey alongside me, never stopping once to complain. You are the love of my life; my pillar of strength and my very best friend. I am eternally grateful that we found each other.

As it turns out, blood is not always family and family is not always blood. Dallas, Heather, and Lynette - you shaped me. I joke about being raised by a pack of wolves and as I wrote this book, I realized...you were my pack. Thank you for showing me what a family is supposed to look like.

Looking back, I can see how many kind and compassionate people there actually were in my little world. Brian, Loren, and "James", my life would not have been the same without you. Thank you for putting me on your wall.

For my partners in crime Char and Bobbie. You taught me that there are people in this world who will step up and care for you when no one else does. I pray that I had as much of an impact on your lives as you did on mine.

We've all heard the adage, "people are in your life for a reason, even if it's only for a season." Teddi, Tony, and Breanna, thank you for showing me how to take a leap of faith. I will always remember the time we shared.

My brother in Christ, Laran. You are, hands down, one of my best friends. You have been a true brother to me and have shown me what an honest man can bring to friendship. Thank you for seeing me.

Never in a million years did I think a Pastor would speak in to my life. Pastor Jim, though I am but a nameless face in a sea of thousands, you have had a profound impact on my life. Your words, your courage to share your personal story, and your faith have provided me the strength and courage I needed to open my heart to Jesus. From the bottom of my heart, thank you.

The realization that I wasn't alone in my guilt and shame was both emotional and enlightening. Lori W., I will never forget the night you helped me realize that it is okay to be broken. Your story changed my path and opened my eyes. Thank you for letting a stranger cry on your shoulder.

Everyone needs that one person who can look you in the eye and tell you to pull your big girl panties up and deal with it. Duncan, you are my favorite. Thank you for sharing your Friday nights with me.

Sometimes we need a little help to maneuver through this thing called life. Lori J, you are my life coach. I am so very grateful for your expertise in PTSD and your ability to help me heal without a bunch of bull. I am so blessed to have traveled this journey with you by my side.

To my squad, Cindy, Dana, Beth, Stacey, Lynne & Elizabeth. You have all taught me the true meaning of friendship. I'm not sure that I would have completed this book without the six of you by my side. Thank you for your love and patience.

Finally, for all my readers whose lives I hope to touch. This book has been a difficult journey; one I almost wasn't prepared to travel. What I want you to take away from this is that you are worthy; you are loved; and you are a WARRIOR. Never give up; have faith in yourself; and always remember that you are NOT alone.

LEGAL DISCLAIMER

DEDICATION

To Wayne.
You saved my life. I wish I could have saved yours.

"Words have no power to impress the mind without the exquisite horror of their reality." Edgar Allan Poe

PROLOGUE

The dirt paths that weaved through the headstones were lined with tow trucks. This was not a new sight for me. It was, however, the last of many funerals I would attend in a tow truck. His was different. I found myself, for the first time, playing the role of spectator. I was watching from the outside as if I were an impostor. I was present but in a dream like state. I noticed dynamics I had never noticed before; the flaws and insecurities of the "popular crowd". A crowd I had once considered myself a part of. One I suddenly wanted nothing to do with.

I stood back in the shadows and watched while this group of people I once considered family, gathered around his casket. He was in his early twenties. He left behind a beautiful young wife, two small children, a sister, and two loving parents. None of them could have ever prepared for the decision he made that changed the course of their lives forever. Most viewed his decision as cowardly and selfish. The aftermath of his decision had a catastrophic effect on his family. The affect it had on me, was life altering.

I understood his pain and had great empathy for what he must have been feeling. Though I do not know the full story that led to his decision, I knew enough to be confident that he and I shared some of the same thoughts and feelings about our lives. I only wish we had been friends instead of competitors. Perhaps then I could have been there for him while he maneuvered through his brokenness. Nonetheless, he was gone, and in a sea of people who simply could not wrap their heads around such a selfish act, I understood completely and forgave him easily. Ironically, taking his own life may very well have saved mine.

When I left the reception and headed back toward the shop to turn in my truck, I was numb. I had no idea that day what my future held. I had no plans to make a drastic change. No plans to pursue faith. Certainly, no plans to lose the very person I had spent my entire life trying to impress. On that day, I had no idea that in two weeks, I would take a giant leap of faith and that I would, once again, be a brave girl.

PART ONE

MONSTERS ARE REAL

"The real world is where the monsters are." ~ Rick Riordan

CHAPTER 1
MONSTERS ARE REAL

"Start by telling me why you're here." She said in a soft and caring voice. Her office was comfortable yet uncomfortable. I hadn't been to therapy in years. I had just come out of a two-week major depressive episode. My chiropractor had given me her number and though I trusted him whole heartedly, I wondered if she was any good. She was younger than me and I worried that she wouldn't understand me because of our age difference.

The question she should have asked was if I was willing to tell her the truth about the monsters that plagued me. I had never told anyone the truth before. Even though I was forty years old, I still held fear that she would judge me, ridicule me, or worse, reject me. I had no idea how to answer her question or where to begin.

****

When I was four years old, my life was what I thought to be normal. Summer became my favorite season as I experienced joy most days. My family lived in a quiet old neighborhood in Las Cruces, New Mexico. Our house was one of many brown, brick, ranch-style homes that lined our peaceful street. Located directly across from our home was a field that was host to a sea of tall brown weeds and was littered with sunflowers. The front of each home was occupied by plush green, square lawns, split down the middle with gray, concrete walkways that led to the front doors. Parallel to the street, there ran a long sidewalk that seemed to have no end. I often imagined that it would lead to an enchanted forest, if ever I were allowed to go exploring. Some of the homes displayed beautiful flowers as a lining to their walkways. That was how I discovered my love for petunias, tulips, and the color purple. During the summer months, everyone in the neighborhood could be found out front at one point or another throughout the day. The children would play and ride their bikes in the street. The adults would gather on the long sidewalk and discuss the highlights of their day. Almost every afternoon we would hear the delightful melody of the ice cream truck as it traveled slowly from house to house. It seemed as if nothing could corrupt the sense of security I felt, not even when my older brother set the field on fire.

The inside of our house was small but cozy, decorated in browns and greens which was normal for the late 1970's. The layout was basic, and our furniture was moderate. My sister and I shared a small room but neither of us required much space at the time and I don't recall ever feeling unhappy about it. The house smelled of Pine-Sol and homemade bread which was soothing to me. There was a set of sliding glass doors in the dining room that led to our backyard. Those doors were only one of two things that I was afraid of when I was four years old. My fascinating imagination had conjured up multiple scenarios whereby I was squished in between the sliding glass doors with no one around to rescue me. But that didn't stop me from conquering them when I wanted to go out and play. I typically only went out back when my sister was at the neighbor's house. They had a trampoline that she enjoyed jumping on, but I was too little, and Mom wouldn't let me go. My sisters' bicycle was kept on the back porch and on the days that she was on the trampoline, I would overthrow the sliding glass doors and go sit on it. I could see her jumping on the trampoline from where I sat. Each time her head poked over the tall wooden fence, I yelled to her, "Look at me, I'm riding your bike". She simply laughed and kept jumping. This made me laugh as well. I was blissfully unaware of the world outside of our neighborhood.

My dad was building his towing and recovery business, so he was gone most days and long into the nights. He was the second thing I was afraid of when I was four years old. He had a gruff, loud voice and when he got angry, everyone in his path was in trouble. For as long as I can remember, it was never a good idea to make Dad mad. His temper was unpredictable. My mom would use our fear of him to her advantage in disciplinary situations. "I'm going to tell your father" was her standard threat and it almost always worked. I don't ever remember a time when I wasn't afraid of Dad.

My mom worked from home and I often spent my days asking her impossible questions. When she had enough of me, she would insist that my sister take me out to play. If my sister wasn't around, Mom would pull out my treasured coloring books and crayons to occupy me. I cherished the waxy smell of the crayons and the sweet, musky smell of a brand-new coloring book. I would get consumed by my crusade to stay between the lines. It was a craft that engaged me for hours. One that I was very passionate about. One hot summer day, my sweet books had disappeared, and I was devastated. To comfort me and shift my focus, my sister convinced me to go with her to the neighbor's house and play. As we walked down the long sidewalk, we noticed fragments of paper scattered across the squares of grass between our house and theirs. Upon closer examination, we discovered that the paper was in fact, the remnants of my beloved coloring books. I was dismayed and immediately ran home to tell my mom. I sat on the couch crying as I watched her march out the front door, a stern look upon her face. Curious, I wiped the tears from my cheeks and followed. Somehow, she had figured out that it was the neighbor girls who had taken my books and ripped them to shreds. She approached the neighbor's mother and scolded her the way she often scolded us when we behaved badly. Though still heartbroken by my four-year-old catastrophe, I felt a sense of justice as I listened to my mother defend me. I believed, in that moment, that my mom would protect me from anything.

Summer came to an end and the holidays quickly approached. My parents started engaging in frequent quiet conversations. I knew something was happening, but I didn't care much about what it was. All that mattered at the time was that Santa was coming and I was going to get new coloring books and toys. We decorated the house together as a family. Dad played and wrestled with us on the floor as Mom rearranged the ornaments us kids had bunched together. And on Christmas Eve, I was convinced that I saw Santa Claus. Just before bed, my brother, my sister, and I were standing at the window in our bedroom. My brother pointed toward the sky, bringing my attention to a bright light that was moving slowly through the clouds. "It's Santa!" he exclaimed. At that same moment, I heard the distinct jingle of sleigh bells. I was overjoyed and went to bed in a euphoric state. It seemed like nothing could disturb the feelings of wholeness four-year-old me had come to embrace.

My parents had been building their business since before I was born. It was a twenty-four hours per day, seven days per week, three hundred and sixty-five days per year, towing and recovery business. My dad had glorious dreams for the company's future and unfortunately, our quiet neighborhood did not align with them. We needed property; something that could grow with the business. So, not long after Christmas, my parents started to include us in those frequent, quiet conversations. They took us to see a house they had found and wanted to buy. I'll never forget that house. It was an eerie, two story, single family home that sat on a busy street yet, had one and a half acres of land in the back. There were two driveways on either side of the house; one was dirt and the other, concrete. My parents would eventually block off the entrance to the concrete driveway with a rope and leave the dirt road open for business access. There was a steep set of stairs that led out of the back of the house to the dirt and weed acreage. There wasn't a patio or a fenced back yard to play in. The front yard was split by a wide concrete sidewalk and closed off by a three-foot chain-link fence. The front porch was covered and extended the length of the front room. At the side of the house, where the porch ended, there was a three-foot drop that led to the long concrete driveway. Someone had stacked cinder blocks at the bottom of the drop to act as stairs. On the other side of the concrete driveway was a yard that was just as long. Some parts were grass and some parts were dirt. The chain link fence on that side, was lined with trees which offered a small amount of privacy. My parents promised they would buy me a swing set for that area. It provided me little solace.

There was something about the front yard that left me uncomfortably vulnerable. There seemed to be little safeguard between the house and the busy street where cars moved past continuously. It wasn't quiet, the neighbors weren't close, and none of the houses looked the same. The area was industrial and despite the numerous homes on the street, there were just as many businesses. Instead of a sidewalk that led to enchanted forests, there was a drainage ditch that led to the nearest waterway. It was full of craw-dads and crickets and other detestable things. If there were any kids in the area, we weren't going to find them playing in the busy street and I was certain I would never hear the delightful melody of the ice cream truck again.

The inside of the house did not offer a feeling of comfort. Instead, it was cold and unwelcoming. It appeared tattered and in need of abundant repair. The dining room and the living room were open and offered a less claustrophobic feel than the tiny, cramped kitchen. The two bedrooms on the main floor were of average size, however, they both had two sizable windows, one on each outer wall. My parents explained to us that my sister and I would share the bedroom at the front of the house. The very concept left me anxious and terrified because of the big windows. My imagination soared as I conjured up many scenarios of scary monsters coming in through them and getting me.

The second floor had a curious layout. As we ascended the stairs, we could turn either right or left. There was an open hall on each side that led back to a single room. This would become my brothers' room. The drop from the hallways to the stairwell was surrounded with a rickety wood fence. The flooring was made of wood but was painted chrome gray and creaked as we walked on it. Inset in the walls of each open hallway were three small doors that allowed access to attic space. It held an ominous feel and the large bay windows, lacking adequate caulking, left the area cold and murky.

The basement was unfinished and unimpressive to my little mind, but my parents saw potential and were enthusiastic at the notion of completing a remodel. At the very back of the house, behind the minuscule kitchen, was an extension that was closed off by what had once been an outer window and an outer door. It was that extension that had elicited my parent's excitement and consideration of that particular house. That space would be used as an office. The one and a half acres in the back, would be used for vehicle storage. It was precisely what they needed to make my dad's dream come true.

The adults talked when we were done with our tour. I sat at the bottom of the stairs that led to the creepy, second floor. I was wearing a pea green, puffy, winter coat, that exhibited a hood lined with faux-fur. Melancholy descended over me as I pulled the furry hood over my head and leaned against the wall. As I eavesdropped on the adult's conversation, I somehow knew that my life would never be the same. There was no doubt we were leaving the comfort of our cookie cutter neighborhood when we left the eerie house later that night.

We moved to the new house early in the summer of 1981. I had just turned five and my birthday was less than exciting. We were all too busy putting the house together and getting organized to celebrate birthdays. My parents were cheerful and content about the change, but I was apprehensive. As my parents began the process of moving the business into the new space, my sister and I found ourselves overcome with boredom. We decided we wanted to go exploring so my sister convinced my mom to let us travel the dirt roadway to the very end. My sister had a way of convincing people to do things. That was one of the many traits I envied about her. Once my mother said yes, we were off. We discovered that the dirt road ended where miles of beautiful fields began. Upon exploration of the open land, we discovered the train tracks and the coal that had fallen from the cars that traveled that route. It seemed necessary to pick up a piece of coal each time we went there. Every day was a new adventure as we explored and discovered new areas. There were patches of beautiful flowers and remnants of old brick structures strewn throughout the terrain. It was magical and something I looked forward to. Though I missed our quiet neighborhood, the fields helped me to establish a sense that everything was going to be okay in this strange environment.

Eventually summer came to an end and it was time to go to school. My brother was entering Junior High, my sister was entering fourth grade, and I was entering Kindergarten. My parents were so consumed with the business that my sister was left with the task of helping ease my anxiety about starting school. I had come to rely on the camaraderie she and I shared. She was my best friend and my only confidant. I had no desire to venture outside of the house unless she was with me and going to school meant being without her. She was in full day school and I would only be going for half the day. She promised me that I would make friends and assured me that it was going to be okay. I was a bashful girl and felt awkward around new people. Within the first few days of school, kids began to pick on me and tease me. They made fun of me because of what my parents did for a living. Until then, I had never considered that I should be ashamed by my parents' business. But there I was, one week in to Kindergarten feeling ashamed and beneath all my classmates. I promptly began hating school and would count down the minutes until it was time to leave. I would push my way to the front of the line at the end of each day and run to the car without looking back. But as time went on and business began to pick up, my mom progressively showed up later and later; prolonging my time spent with the mean kids. Within a few short weeks, the day came when my mom forgot me. I was humiliated as I watched the last kid get picked up. When I sat down to wait, my feelings were confirmed. Normal, as I knew it, was no longer.

I sat on the cold, concrete steps that led to the small cottage of my kindergarten. My head was leaning on my left hand which was propped up on my left leg. Both my legs swayed back and forth as I pretended that the long brown stick in my right hand was writing something on the concrete. A gentle wind picked up, causing my hair to fall over my face; hiding my tears. My teacher poked her head out the door of my classroom and told me that someone was on their way to get me. I was unusually aware of the sounds that afternoon; birds chirping, leaves on the trees rustling, the wind whistling, grasshoppers singing and the grass swaying back and forth in motion with my legs. After what seemed like an eternity, I finally heard the sounds I had been waiting for. The distinctive sounds of the transmission moving from gear to gear to gain speed up the street and the rattling of chains. Through the trees, I saw the tow truck, my chauffeur for the four-block ride home. I yelled to the teacher that he was there, wiped my tear stained face, and ran down the long sidewalk to greet the driver. I don't remember his name, but that day, he was my savior. Within a minute, we pulled onto the long dirt road that ran parallel to my house. I jumped out of the truck and ran up the steep wooden steps to the office. My mom was busy on the phone and didn't acknowledge me or the fact that she had forgotten me at school. Disappointed, I went inside the house to start on my chores. My sister wouldn't be home for a couple of hours, so I was on my own. After that it became common place for one of the drivers to pick me up after school, and it was not unusual for them to be late.

A couple of weeks went by and I decided that I would venture out front to play in the dirt patch that was off the front porch next to the wide sidewalk. It was a good way to kill time while I waited for my sister to get home from school and I would be able to see her walking from the bus stop. I was anxious as I sat by myself while so many strangers passed by in their cars. But I wanted desperately to see my sister, so I remained seated on the ground. I sang to myself as I played in the dirt. Almost as if out of nowhere, two men in an old sixties model Chevrolet pickup truck pulled up in front of the chain link fence. An older man with a bald head and a long beard got out of the passenger side door. He held a rope in his right hand and reached over the fence with his left; attempting to unlock the gate that blocked him from the sidewalk. He stared me straight in the eyes from the moment he exited the vehicle to the time he approached the gate. He had a strange smile on his face, and he laughed as he exclaimed, "Now I've got you!". I ran into the house and went straight to the office to get my mom. Fear consumed my body and I was shaking as I told her what had happened. She walked with me to the front door to investigate. After looking through the window and observing that the men were no longer there, she made sure the door was locked, told me not to go back outside, and went back to work. I sat nervously on the couch while I waited for my sister to get home, periodically peeking out the front window to see if the men were back. I refused to go out front again unless my sister was with me. She was the only person who took the time to comfort me and vow her protection over me.

Not long after that incident, my sister and I went on a quest to find other kids on our street. We knew that there were kids our age directly across the street from us, however, for some reason, they were not allowed to play with us. As a result of the teasing both my sister and I had been receiving at school, we assumed their parents didn't want them around the tow truck drivers' daughters. We had to be careful as we explored, walking as close to the ditch as possible to avoid collision with all the cars. Our exploration paid off when we met a girl down the street. She was playing in her yard with her younger brother. She was about my age, long black hair, and beautiful. She was dressed nice and spoke like she was older. We walked back and forth in front of her house a couple of times before she ran up to the fence and asked us who we were and where we came from. Her name was Maddie Arke. She didn't seem to care what our parents did for a living and the three of us rapidly became inseparable. We discovered that Maddie and I both went to the same Kindergarten, but she was in the other class. Her Mom worked as a nurse and her dad was retired military, so he stayed home with the kids. Our parents insisted on meeting since we were spending so much time together. They too became fast friends and within weeks, we were spending most of our time at the Arke's. It was the perfect arrangement for my parents. The business was demanding every second of their time, so it made life easier on them to send us over to Maddie's house. I was delighted to have a friend and time spent with her lessened the sadness I felt from moving.

Despite the many changes and my deep fear of what waited beyond the chain link fence, I was starting to settle in and feel like maybe a new "normal" had returned. My sister and I would spend hours almost every day hanging out with Maddie after our chores were done. Her Mom would take us to parks and museums after school and her dad would often cook us dinner. There was a clear sense of trust and acceptance between the two families. By the time I was six, both families operated almost as if we were one cohesive unit. I was enjoying our new life despite the confirmation of why the windows in our bedroom were so scary. We had watched the movie Poltergeist one Saturday evening. Sometime late in the night, the winds kicked up and a branch from the large oak tree outside our window came crashing through it. My sister screamed and I, paralyzed as the movie replayed in my head, cowered under the covers. I have never been able to watch scary movies since.

Mr. Arke was an older man; much older than Mrs. Arke. He was shorter than my dad and a little overweight. His skin was dark, and he had round, beady eyes that looked black most of the time. He smelled of cheap cologne and Cuban cigars. He whistled and hummed when he was occupied with a task. He didn't talk much but he was always watching, expending most of his energy and attention on the kids. He portrayed himself as a loving and attentive father who catered to his daughter and all her friends.

One Saturday night, my parents had Mr. Arke come over to watch us while they went out to dinner. My sister, Mr. Arke, and I were in the front room watching television. I sat on the grey and black striped cloth couch; my sister sat on the pastel striped cloth chair; Mr. Arke was sitting in my dad's brown leather recliner. We were forbidden to sit in Dad's recliner but sometimes, when he wasn't around, I would sneak over there and enjoy the comfort of the leather and the smell of Dad's cologne. Mr. Arke asked me to come sit on his lap. I jumped at the opportunity to be in Dad's chair. After climbing up in to his lap, we sat for a few minutes and watched tv. He abruptly pulled me back toward him and began vigorously rubbing my vagina through my jeans. I panicked and began to scream for him to stop. He laughed and told me to be quiet, but I refused to comply. I kept screaming "Stop" and fighting him, desperately trying to get away. My sister sat, frozen in the chair, watching in horror. He got angry with me and sent me to my room. I gladly fled with tears in my eyes. As I ran from him, I caught a glimpse of my brother's shadow in the doorway out of the corner of my eye. I didn't call out to him. I just ran to my bedroom, desperate to escape Mr. Arke. I was confused and scared; I didn't have a clear understanding of what had just happened. I knew what Mr. Arke had done was wrong. What he did was the precise reason my mom made us wear shorts under our skirts. But I was in jeans and still, he touched me. As I lay there waiting for my sister, I froze with every creak of the floor outside my door. Paralyzed in fear, it never occurred to me that I had just left my sister, alone, with a monster.

Upon wakening the next morning, my sister and I agreed that we would go to our mother together and tell her what Mr. Arke had done. My mother was in the kitchen, preparing breakfast and humming to herself. We began the conversation by informing her that Mr. Arke was a pervert. She became angry and scolded us for saying something so mean about such a nice man. She further scolded us for being so ungrateful of him helping and how horrible of us to try and ruin our dad's closest friendship. She told us that we dare not tell Dad or he would be very angry with us. That was that. We were not to bring it up again.

In that moment, the same mother who fought for my honor over coloring books, turned cold and callous. Butterflies emerged in my stomach and my heart began to bleed. We were instructed to start setting the table for breakfast as if our conversation hadn't happened. I remained quiet and humble as I went about my day. The confusion I experienced the night before was swallowed whole by insecurity. My mother's rejection promptly bred doubt and mistrust inside of me. I was insignificant; disposable absent perfection.

It was a decade later when I learned that my mother had been warned by other neighbors in the area when we moved there. She had been told that Mr. Arke was believed to be a pedophile and she was warned to keep her daughters away from him. Despite those warnings and despite our attempt at telling her our story, she chose not to listen.

CHAPTER 2
A NEW NORMAL

Christina wasn't like other therapists I had in the past. She focused on teaching me techniques to combat the constant thoughts and nightmares. She was more like a life coach than a therapist. The uncertainty I felt our first session was quickly replaced with confidence. I knew, in my gut, that I could tell Christina anything and she wouldn't reject me.

****

I lived in constant fear during the weeks following the incident with Mr. Arke. I worried that I had somehow provoked him. I shouldn't have sat on his lap. My mother was so angry that I thought I had done something wrong. We continued to spend the same amount of time at the Arke's, as if nothing had happened. When at home, I did my best to make my mother happy, even doing extra chores to show her that I was extra good. I began to have difficulty sleeping and was plagued with nightmares. I didn't understand why Mr. Arke did what he did. I only knew the fear that consumed me and the whisper in my ear telling me that he was dangerous. My innate instinct to fight was the only thing that kept me from being raped by him. This I knew for sure. My mother had always been explicit with us about inappropriate sexual contact, so I was well aware of the dangers that lurked from men. I learned quickly how to protect myself from Mr. Arke and allowed instinct to be my guide.

The Arke's house was small, much smaller than ours. It was a ranch style home with a kitchen, a living room, three small bedrooms and a small bathroom. There was no basement and no real storage to speak of. Their yard was larger than the entire house making it stand out like a sore thumb on the busy street. When I went to their house, I would enter through the back door which led directly to the kitchen. There was a window next to that door and on nice days, it was almost always open. As I ventured through the back yard, my senses would kick in to high gear. I would listen for noise coming from the kitchen; I would smell for his cologne; I would pay attention to the feeling in my gut. If I heard noises in the kitchen, I knew that it was most likely him and I would be on high alert from the moment I opened the door. If it was silent, I knew to proceed with caution and that he would likely be sitting in his wooden, rocking, swivel chair. Regardless of his location within the house, I instinctively knew to keep myself facing him at all times; never turn my back and allow myself to be vulnerable. No one taught me that. I just knew it; deep to my core. I knew that he was bad, and I knew that no one was going to protect me from him but me.

Every time I entered their house, I prepared myself for battle. Upon seeing him, I crossed my arms in front of my body, looked him straight in the eye and cursed at him. I would press my back up against the wall and walk sideways toward the hall. He always laughed at me and never blinked or broke eye contact. Once I moved past the small, hall closet, I practically ran to Maddie's room. If Mrs. Arke or the kids were in the same room as him, I would project my best death stare to make sure he knew I wasn't going to let him hurt me again. No matter what the situation, I didn't let my guard down. He simply laughed or mouthed inappropriate things to me but he seemed to know that I wasn't going to go down without a fight and so he left me be. My parents had come to rely on the Arke's to help care for me by making sure I got to and from the bus stop. During the winter months, Mr. Arke would take us to and from school in his creepy passenger van. Each day, I experienced stress and anxiety as I prepared for school. I frequently suffered from stomach aches and would try anything to stay home or convince my mom that she needed to take me. But nothing I said persuaded her. Day after day, it was me against the monster.

I found myself in turmoil over my desire to keep my friendship with Maddie. She was one of the popular girls and since she was nice to me, it meant that the other kids didn't tease me as much. When she would invite me over for a sleepover, I would experience an internal conflict that was generally settled by six-year-old logic. I wanted a friend and I wanted to belong. I had been successfully preventing Mr. Arke from hurting me so sleeping over at one of the popular girls' house always outweighed the stress and anxiety that I experienced. Sleep overs were more complex than the daily visits. I would make sure that I packed full pajamas that covered my entire body. I would only use the bathroom when Mr. Arke was busy, and I refused to obey his toilet paper rule. We were allowed only two sheets to wipe with after we had finished our business. I didn't understand his reasoning for the rule back then; I simply knew that it didn't make sense to me because that never seemed enough to dry me off. I would smile to myself as I sat on the toilet and counted out eight sheets of paper. It felt like a small victory, though I didn't fully understand what it was I was conquering. When bedtime came, Maddie and I would argue over who got to sleep on the inside of the bed. Due to the size of Maddie's room, her bed was flush with the wall to make room for her dresser and night stand. I had determined that if I slept on the inside, with her on the outside, I would be safe. He would have to climb over her to get to me and somehow, I just knew that the chances of that were slim. Though reluctant, Maddie would always give in to me. Just before lights out, Mr. Arke would peer into the room to say good night. He would always have a smirk on his face that was illuminated by the hall light. I would cower behind Maddie and didn't dare make eye contact with him. Sleep there was broken and only came in small spurts throughout the night. When morning arrived, I had triumphed and the courage to sleep over again would build inside me.

By the time I turned seven, I was confident in my abilities to avoid another incident with Mr. Arke. Protecting myself had become part of the new normal though it had its downfalls. I was older than the other kids my age. I understood and thought about topics that should have been saved for adolescence or adulthood. Most prevalent was the fact that I had become very aware of female sexuality. On family movie nights, my dad would choose a Rated R movie that was playing on Cinemax; movies that, in the 80's, dangerously crossed the line into pornography. I found myself extremely uncomfortable and embarrassed when the sex scenes started. I silently wished my dad would change the channel and would feel intense relief when the scene ended, and I could open my eyes. Though, closing my eyes didn't make the sounds dissipate. The movies left me excited and shameful at the same time. I experienced sadness and was guilt ridden for having even watched them. But movie night was the rare occurrence when we were able to spend time with Dad. By then, the business kept him away most nights and I missed wrestling on the floor and laughing with him. So, I would take movie night, even if it meant two hours of periodic discomfort.

Though I loved him with all my soul, my dad, unfortunately, was raised in an era when being sexist wasn't considered wrong. It was made very clear, at the age of seven, that a girl's job was to take care of the house, the children, cook, and take care of the man. It was the man's job to work and bring home the money. Children were to be seen and not heard and women were to comply with whatever demands were placed on them. This was simply how it was. Mom would spend an hour in the bathroom, every morning, applying facial creams and makeup. She always dressed pretty, making sure to accentuate her beautiful figure. She wore two-inch, spiked high heels almost every day; even if she was wearing jeans. It was always important that she looked beautiful for my dad. I would watch in fascination every morning as she covered her beautiful face with layer upon layer of makeup. She would explain the importance of each step and then go on to educate me about her nighttime ritual which I rarely had occasion to see. She would preach to me about proper posture and made me walk around the house with a heavy book on my head. It was important, if I ever wanted to be a model like she once was. I wanted to be as beautiful as my mom and as sexy as the women in the movies. That was how I would find a good man like my dad.

We kept a set of binoculars close to the dining room table. On the rare occasion that my dad was home for dinner, he would sit at the head of the table, facing a window that had a clear view of our neighbor's house. Our neighbor was an older gentleman whose twenty-something daughter visited him on a regular basis. She was very pretty and was always friendly with us. During the spring and summer months, she would sunbath in a bikini on the side of their house. It was commonplace for my dad to ask my mom to hand him the binoculars so he could watch her while we ate. He would make suggestive comments about her body and hand the binoculars to my brother so he could look too. This prompted me to look at myself in the mirror and wonder what I would look like in a bikini, though, my mother would never allow me to buy one. She said it was inappropriate for a girl to wear a bikini because it was too revealing. But the neighbor girl always wore one and Maddie wore them too. I didn't understand why I couldn't have one because it would make me look older and sexy. I thought that's what girls were supposed to be like.

Despite the messages I was receiving about sexuality, home was the only place I felt safe when I was seven years old. The time before and after school was spent avoiding Mr. Arke; my time at school was spent overhearing whispers of the other kids talking bad about me because of my parent's business. Even hanging out with Maddie didn't completely stop their malicious comments. But when I was home, I could relax and hang out with my sister. Sometimes, when our chores were done, we would play library in our room and have fun for hours. Time spent with my sister meant time spent being a normal kid. It was my only opportunity to let the worries slip away. It was the one place I could still allow curiosity to take over.

Upstairs, where the wood floors creaked and the air was murky, the outside of my brothers' room was host to a mess of boxes. One of them was filled to the brim with Penthouse and Playboy magazines. There were times when I would sneak up there to peek inside at what I knew wasn't meant for such young eyes. I was captivated by the beautiful women inside. The feelings that permeated throughout my body were both exciting and shameful. Something about them fascinated me. I wanted to be like the women spread out across those glossy pages. They had the attention of every man that happened upon them; attention I longed for and felt I needed. I was always overcome with tremendous guilt and shame when I snuck back downstairs. I wholeheartedly believed that I needed to be like the women in those books in order to receive love from a man.

My brother had quite a few friends and they would always hang out upstairs. One of them was fifteen years old and we didn't see him much. He was always getting in trouble, so my brother couldn't have him over often. When he did come around, he was always nice to me and I didn't believe him to be a trouble maker. On one occasion, he convinced me to go upstairs and hang out with them. I was excited at the notion of hanging out with the big kids, so I happily went along. After a while, my brother fell asleep, but we stayed up and talked. When it came time for bed, he asked me to lay down with him. It felt good to belong and I didn't think twice before I said yes. And, when he asked me to give him a hand job, I did it. It didn't seem wrong to me at the time. In fact, when I finished, or, rather, when he finished, I asked him what he was going to do for me. He seemed disgusted and got angry with me. He ordered me to leave but I questioned him. I had done what he asked and didn't understand why that upset him so badly. I finally fled to my room and cried myself to sleep. We never spoke of it and I didn't tell anyone. I was ashamed and guilt ridden, confused by my feelings. Suddenly, the one place that was safe, wasn't.

By the time I entered second grade, I was anxious and suffering from chronic stomach aches and insomnia. I was afraid to speak up about anything, even telling the teacher that I needed to go to the bathroom paralyzed me. I peed my pants at my desk several times that year and my mom had to bring me a change of clothing every time. It was humiliating and gave the other kids one more insult to add to their ruthless teasing. When I was able to sleep, I endured daunting nightmares. I began sleepwalking and ended up outside on the front porch one night. Everyone, including the doctor, labeled me as a nervous and hyperactive kid. No one asked the hard questions; and I didn't offer up any of the hard answers.

What minimal friendships I had at school dissipated, even Maddie wouldn't hang out with me while we were there. My head was full of grown up thoughts and I struggled to relate to my peers. The only reason Maddie hung out with me outside of school was because our parents expected us to. I would have been perfectly okay to never set foot in her house again. I had become a meek little girl. Afraid to speak up, afraid to speak out, and afraid of what people might say or do to me. I dressed poorly and my hair was always a mess. I had no idea how to care for myself properly and I knew it. Even though I watched my mom make herself pretty every morning, I didn't learn basic hygiene, only basic makeup principals. I wanted to have nice clothes and look as pretty as my classmates, but that wasn't a priority for my parents. They were busy with the business and money was always sparse. It became easier to wear the outdated hand me downs and let my hair do whatever it wanted to do. Fighting with my mom about it was pointless; I could never win.

Halfway through my second-grade year, a girl named Emily Rose came up to me at recess. Everyone knew who she was. She had been held back a year and had a reputation of being mean. Which, somehow, made her cool. I was playing on the monkey bars by myself when she walked up and announced that she felt sorry for me, so she decided that she was going to be my friend. Emily Rose was tall, like me. She had thin, short, blonde hair and was always tan, as if she came straight off a California beach. She was pretty, despite the awkwardly large size of her ears. She was dressed nice and already wore make up. I looked her up and down and realized that she was probably the same size as me. I wondered what her closet looked like. And for some reason, I felt sorry for her too. She seemed sad underneath the tough girl facade and I felt like I could relate to her. She wasn't like the other kids; her mind seemed older like mine. I ignored her crass announcement and agreed to be her friend. She was the only one offering, and I thought it would be nice to have access to her wardrobe.

Emily Rose and I quickly became inseparable. She constantly insulted my clothing, my hair, my face, and my weight. Rather than get upset by it, I asked her to help me be pretty like the women on television. She was delighted by my request. It was the beginning of a bona fide toxic relationship. One that would take me over a decade to end.

CHAPTER 3
BRAVE LITTLE GIRL

Sometime around our third session, Christina looked at me and told me that I was a brave little girl. My face turned a light shade of crimson, I politely smiled and shifted my body uncomfortably. I didn't believe her, but I didn't want to be rude. I'm certain she saw how uncomfortable her statement had made me. Brave was not a word I would ever have used to describe myself. Bad, fat, ugly, fearful, shameful, whore, worthless...these were the words I thought of when I thought of me.

****

By the end of second grade, I was spending less time with Maddie and as much time as possible with Emily Rose. The other kids in my class stopped talking badly about me and almost seemed afraid of me. I was cool for the first time in my young life. My parents bought my sister and I a Mickey Mouse Lamp/Phone so we could talk to our friends at night. That became my new favorite thing to do and it replaced the forced play dates with Maddie. I was still made to go over there before school and Mr. Arke still drove us in inclement weather. But my overall exposure to him was lessened. It was a refreshing break and it provided me the opportunity to relax a little. And while the other girls were playing with barbies, Emily Rose and I spent hours talking about boys, clothes, and how to make me look less ugly. Even though I didn't tell her about Mr. Arke or my brothers' friend, I felt like she understood me. She was my best friend and I was thrilled about that.

As summer approached, my parent's business was growing by leaps and bounds. If Dad was awake, he was working, and Mom spent most of her hours in the office as well. They were always tired and always seemed grumpy. Dad yelled, a lot. He didn't play with us anymore and if he was home, he and Mom were usually in their bedroom with the door shut. If we did see Dad, it was likely because we were in trouble. If we watched a movie on the weekends, it was a rare treat. They were busy all the time and having kids around only added to their stress. At the beginning of summer, they decided to ask my dad's mom to move in to help care for us girls. In order to make that happen, they needed to remodel the upstairs and the basement so that everyone would fit. There was one problem with that though. Having two little girls under foot during construction was not something my parents were willing to finagle. So, they did what they thought would be the best thing ever. They sent my sister and I on a month-long vacation...with the monster.

It was the trip of a lifetime; Disney World in Florida. I was excited but afraid. I had never been away from my parents for more than one night at a time. What if Mr. Arke tried to touch me? Or worse, what if I couldn't protect myself for that long? But it was Disney World; the most magical place on earth. The notion was bittersweet, and I found myself in the depths of anxiety as we prepared to leave.

We set out on an early summer morning in the Arke's family motor home. It was an old, black, motor home with one of those van front ends and a bed over the cab. My stomach was full of butterflies as we drove east into the sunrise. My mind was full of thoughts about Mickey Mouse, roller coasters, beaches, and what to do if Mr. Arke tried to touch me. I memorized the layout of the motor home and calculated the safest place to sleep. There was a table in the back that folded down into a bed. I decided that I would sleep there, with my back to the window, feet facing toward the front. I could see everything from that point in the RV and believed I would have an advantage over Mr. Arke if he dared try to approach me in the night. I took note that the exit door was narrow and the doors to the cab were not easily accessible from inside. I reminded myself that I would need to be mindful of where Mr. Arke was at all times so that I didn't leave myself exposed. Once I had a plan mapped out in my mind, I settled in for the long journey ahead of us.

We traveled slowly from city to city during the day, stopping at campgrounds during the night. My sister, Maddie and I listened to music and played cards to pass the time as we drove. Most of the campgrounds had pools and if we arrived early enough, we would be allowed to go swimming. Maddie had multiple bikinis to choose from while my sister and I each had one, one-piece suit to get us through the duration of the trip. If there was still daylight outside, we would lay out on the deck of the pools and sunbathe. We giggled when we saw cute older boys and Maddie would flirt with them endlessly. I envied her beauty and her boldness. Admittedly, I was jealous and longed to be more like her. She was older than me by about nine months and made sure I was completely aware of that. My eighth birthday was coming up but since she was already eight, she claimed to be more mature than I. We had silly arguments over who oversaw the watch and she always won because she was older. Mr. Arke ridiculed me one night after we arrived back at the motor home late, even though I had begged Maddie to head back because I knew it was time to leave. She smiled coyly as he made fun of me for not knowing how to read a watch. As if seeing me belittled provided her satisfaction. I was pretty sure that Maddie didn't bother my sister because she was so much older than the both of us. It made me sad when she was mean to me but if I complained to Mrs. Arke about it, Maddie's behavior only got worse. It was best to keep my mouth shut and endure whatever torment was bestowed upon me.

During the night hours, I found it difficult to rest and quickly discovered what it meant to sleep with one eye open. One night I watched silently as Mr. Arke reached up to the bed above the cab and grabbed my sisters butt. I wondered why she didn't insist on similar sleeping arrangements as me but concluded that she must have known what she was doing. It was a simple reminder that I could not let my guard down. Though he hadn't blatantly grabbed at me like that, he had brushed his hand against me on several occasions. He constantly mouthed obscenities at me and then laughed when I offered him a look of disgust. Our quarters were tight, and it was more difficult to block myself and curse at him when everyone was so close together. No, rest did not come easy during that trip.

After what seemed like an eternity, we finally made it to Florida. We were all overflowing with excitement and couldn't wait to begin our adventures at Disney World. But I had never been a big fan of amusement parks. Mainly because I suffered motion sickness easily. I was afraid of the roller coasters and wasn't too sure if there were a lot of rides I could bring myself to explore. Honestly, I was more entranced with all the characters and the different lands that came to life before my eyes. I wanted to explore the adventures provided for the little kids but wanted to be with my sister and Maddie at the same time. They wanted nothing to do with the baby stuff and only wanted to explore the big kid rides because that was what was cool. I tried, at first, to stick with them and try out the things they wanted to do. But I rapidly became a nuisance and they complained to Mrs. Arke enough that she scolded me and insisted that I spend my time with Maddie's little brother Stephen. I was torn between wanting to be one of the big kids and wanting to be the little kid that I was. After a short spell of pouting, I complied with Mrs. Arke's request and set off to explore the little kid activities. I was captivated by Fantasyland and easily convinced Stephen to spend our time there. The Mad Tea Party ride was our favorite; we spun in those cups for hours. I was overjoyed each time I saw Alice, Cinderella, and Mickey. We heard the melody of *"It's a Small World"* time and again leaving the words forever engraved in our minds. Our final night in Disney World was spent watching the fireworks cascade over Cinderella Castle. My heart was full and for the first time in what seemed like forever, the weight of my worries slipped away with the exploding colors in the sky.

      After four enchanting days at the best place on earth, we continued our adventure at SeaWorld. I instantly fell in love with Shamu the Whale and wanted nothing more than to sit and watch him jump in and out of the water all day. But the "older girls" were tired of all the baby attractions and wanted only to go to the beach. Though disappointed, I was content to purchase a Shamu stuffed toy and leave the fantasies behind. By this time, it was mid-day and the Arke's announced that we were going to stop at a relative's house. We all groaned in defeat as they explained that the beach would be skipped completely if we complained about the deviation from our schedule. And as imagined, it was a boring detour. My sister and I didn't know anyone and were mostly left alone in the camper for the duration of the two days that we were there. I didn't mind though. She had been spending the better part of her time with Maddie and I was content to have some time with her myself. I took advantage of our time together and expressed my sadness at being left out of the fun that her and Maddie were having together. Given her kind-hearted nature, my sister apologized and promised that she would not abandon me during our beach adventures.

We approached Daytona Beach mid-morning. The sand was jam-packed with people and I imagined it looked like a giant ant farm from space. My attention was quickly redirected when I saw the massive body of blue water. It was like nothing I could have imagined. My eyes were wide with awe as we gathered our beach gear and headed toward the water. Then I saw the ships. Miles out in the ocean were three large gray ships that appeared to stand still in the water. They added a beauty to the ocean that I had not anticipated. I was obsessed with them most of the day and drove my sister crazy as I took picture after picture of the same three ships. I was completely mesmerized by those ships and to this day, I couldn't begin to tell you why.

We spent the next several days at the beach. I wasn't a very good swimmer and spent most of my time building sand castles and watching the ships. If I dared venture in to the water, it was only to prove to my sister and Maddie that I wasn't a baby. To that end, only I suffered for my pride because every time I went in the water, I somehow ended up on my butt with a mouth full of salt and seaweed. The girls would laugh at me and I would angrily return to my safe spot on the beach. During the evening hours, we would venture out to the stores on the piers. Something about the color of the sunset on the ocean as we walked along the pier provided me a sense of peace. It was as if I was someone else, living a different life. So, it was bittersweet when we finally left; I felt turmoil inside me. I was homesick, yet, I wanted this to be home. But it was time to go back and the journey would be a long one. By this time, we were all tired of each other and anxious to get back to our lives.

Though the stops were less frequent on the way back, we did still stop. In Texas, we found a campground that was host to multiple activities and swimming pools. The Arke's decided to stop there for a few days to get everyone out of the motor home. It was nice to get outside and run around. But after two days of spending every waking hour in the sun, I became badly burned. My body was red from head to toe and in some areas, there were blisters. I became very ill and could not stop throwing up. Mrs. Arke got angry at me for vomiting in the toilet of the motor home and scolded me. She told me that if I must throw up, I needed to do it in the sink instead. I didn't understand why she was so mad at me and became afraid to vomit for fear of getting in more trouble. I was miserable and just wanted to go home. My sister and Maddie weren't burnt but I had fairer skin then they did. I was sad and lonely as I spent the remainder of our time there inside the motor home by myself. This allowed Mr. Arke more opportunities to make inappropriate sexual comments to me while Mrs. Arke and the other kids were off at the pool. Sick and exposed, I managed to find the strength to curse at him and berate him. I'm not sure why he didn't take advantage of my weakened state, but I was grateful that his only response was laughter. His chilling, haunting, laughter.

As we began our final decent home, our stops became almost nonexistent and the chatter in the back of the motor home was minimal. We were all tired of the trip and tired of each other. Excitement swelled up inside of me when I saw our city lights in the horizon. What a relief; we were finally back home. I had successfully made it through the trip with the monster. It was as if I was invincible.

The reward for spending a month with the Arke's was a newly remodeled bedroom and new furniture. I finally had my own bed, my own night stand, my own dresser, and my very own desk. As much as I cherished my sister, we had always shared everything, and it was nice to have some things that I could call my own. Going on a month-long journey with the monster seemed a small price to pay for the room and all of its contents. But the thrill of it was short lived. Once Grandma moved in, life only got more difficult to manage. What little childhood excitement I had left inside of me was taken away by her words and was replaced with hopelessness for my future.

CHAPTER 4
STICKS AND STONES

Sticks and stones may break your bones, but words will forever hurt you.

Christina was the first therapist that I was ever completely honest with. I told her everything that I had been holding in for all those years. She never judged me, and she never made me feel like it was my fault. She taught me; she coached me. I had many epiphanies while sitting in her office. She understood why the words hurt so much and why the words still echoed in my head after so many years. She helped me realize that the words were in fact a big part of the problem. It was our fifth session when she handed me a diagnosis I was not prepared for. PTSD. For years I had been told that I was Bipolar and though I always questioned that diagnosis, it was what I became willing to accept. I was confused and perhaps a bit relieved by her conclusion. Could I heal from this? Could I maneuver this better? Could I be normal? My mind was filled with questions but the most prevalent was, how could this be?

****

My Grandmother was five foot three, heavyset, with short, gray, permed hair, round glasses and big breasts. She always wore a muumuu dress and slippers around the house. If she was going out, she would wear pant suits and bright red lipstick. She came to the United States from Italy with her family when she was a small child. She was the only girl in a family of eight and in the early 1900's, that meant that she was left with her mother to care for domestic things, while her brothers attended school and did the fun things that boys could do back then. She would tell us stories of her life when she was little. How she had to educate herself and teach herself English; she was a girl and wasn't given the same opportunities as her brothers. The bitterness in her voice was hard to ignore as she told us her tales. But the life she lived as a young woman more than made up for the shortcomings of her childhood. She boasted of travel around the world and parties and glamour. She was a beautiful young woman who drank a lot and smoked cigarettes like the stars of Hollywood. Yet, she proclaimed her devotion to God as a faithful Catholic woman. She was intelligent and made sure everyone knew it. Being around Grandma was a double-edged sword. Her stories of struggle and triumph made my heart ache for her. But her arrogance and her contemptuous attitude toward me made me hate her more.

For as long as I can remember, Grandma made sure that I knew I wasn't baptized like my sister and brother. She would take me to church on Sundays and special events at the church on weeknights. She and her friends would discuss my impurity and how I was destined to an eternity in hell. All the while, I would sit quietly and listen in horror as my inevitable fate was sealed by the ladies of the Catholic Church. I didn't understand why I wasn't baptized but somehow felt as though it was my fault. God didn't want me, and I concluded that must have been why God didn't protect me. Grandma and her friends made no attempts to educate me or assure me that none of it was my doing. This left me hating God, hating Catholics, and hating Grandma even more. She seemed to hate me too, for what reason, I do not know. But when we returned from our month-long trip with the monster, she had moved in and my young little life became more of a battle than it was before. Something I didn't realize was possible.

Everything I did seemed to trigger Grandma in ways I did not understand. She had no experience with little girls since all her children were boys. And suddenly, she was tasked with caring for two of them. One of which was quite compliant and baptized. The other, was me. Grandma complained about everything I did. Every. Single. Thing. Each day after school, I was to complete my chores, just as I had done for years. Once Grandma was inspecting my work, it was never satisfactory. She would consistently tell me that I hadn't done it correctly and would make me do it again. Up until then, I had only known one way to clean a toilet and one way to make my bed. She would complain to my parents that I was lazy and encourage them to punish me. They always did. I spent more time grounded than not. At first, I tried to meet her expectations, but it didn't seem as though I could. In my young mind, I believed that nothing I did would be enough for her. By the time I was nine, I succumbed to the idea that I could do nothing right in the eyes of Grandma.

By this time, we didn't see much of the Arke's anymore. Every now and then, Mr. Arke would try to give me a ride to or from school if it was cold out, but I would decline. Just the sight of him would make me cringe as he smiled smugly and looked my body up and down. Walking to and from the bus stop had become the only solace in my days. Often, after school, I would take my walk home as an opportunity to separate myself from any good feelings I might have been having and would allow melancholy to take over. I had learned early on that it was easier to bring myself to the dark place than to allow Grandma to do it. For some reason, when she did it, it hurt more.

Time and again I would lie and say that I had homework so I would be excused from spending any extra time with Grandma. I would escape to my room and sit at my desk, staring at blank pieces of paper. If anyone happened up the stairs, I would open a book and pretend to write something. I became quite talented at faking it. The time I spent in my room was consumed with dreams of a different life. I imagined myself as a beautiful woman, rescued from my childhood hell by Prince Charming. I imagined a daughter of my own, one who would be loved and cared for the way I had longed to be loved and cared for. Sadness would overcome me when my fantasies were interrupted by reality. Dinner became my most dreaded meal of the day. While we helped Grandma prepare our meal and set the table, she would chastise me for anything and everything. Oh, I would try to tune her out, but often, the words she spoke cut so deep, there was no way I could avoid the injury.

By the age of nine, I believed that I was a fat, ugly, cow. Though I was tall and thin, Grandma and Emily Rose made sure I knew that they perceived me to be fat and ugly. I did like to eat, after all, I was growing quickly and unfortunately, I was hitting puberty early. But I was far from fat or ugly and my energy and metabolism were terrific. But, if I was the first to start serving myself at the dinner table, Grandma would tell me I was being a pig and that if I continued to eat like that, I was going to get fatter. I was ashamed of myself and often lost my appetite immediately following her words. I would force myself to eat while holding back tears. Luckily, we weren't allowed to speak at the dinner table so I could stare at my plate and easily hide my feelings. I began to experience discomfort when eating in front of other people, especially classmates. Surely if my own grandmother thought I was a pig, the kids I went to school with would think the same. Emily Rose was brutal and would simply lecture me about my overall ugliness the entire time we ate lunch. I held on to every word that she and my Grandmother said to me. No one was telling me anything to contradict those opinions, so I concluded that I was fat, ugly, and had no fashion sense. Dreams of Prince Charming were eventually replaced with hope of becoming a sexy super model that all men would fawn over. I had concluded that the power of beauty and sex were what mattered in the realm of men and women. My weight, looks, and fashion choices became the sole focus of my thoughts.

By the time I turned ten, Grandma continued to berate me and consistently reminded me that I wasn't good enough. If I was daydreaming and taking too long to do my chores, she would scold me and tell me how lazy I was. If I ate something outside of meal times, she would caution me to watch my weight. If I dared to complain to my mother, I would only face more scolding and would be told to simply do what was asked of me and be nicer to Grandma. I didn't dare say anything to Dad. His presence at home had become scarce and if he was there, it was only to eat, sleep, and discipline. It seemed that all he did was yell and nothing, even doing what was asked and being nice, stopped his outbursts. Fear consumed me when he was around and though I made every attempt to portray perfection, it was never enough. I found myself grateful for his absence most days. Only during the night hours did I grieve for the dad I once had. But I didn't dare share my feelings with anyone...not even my most trusted confidant. Grandma wasn't nearly as dreadful toward my sister. I never blamed her though. She was just a child and her personality wasn't one of arrogance. If I did happen to complain about the way Grandma treated me, my sister simply listened with great empathy and kindness. It was hard to be mad at her for anything when she always treated me so well. She knew that Grandma made my life difficult and tried to teach me how to overcome it. But by then, I didn't want to listen. I was ten years old, going through puberty, and my mind was full of adult thoughts and feelings that I didn't understand. Rebellion began to run through me, and I only wanted to punish my Grandmother for all the terrible things that had happened to me.

By the end of fifth grade, I had made a couple of new friends at school. Girls that were built like me; tall, already filling out, and a bit boy crazy. I didn't dare tell them about the magazines I often viewed and kept my mouth shut tight about Mr. Arke and my brother's friend. I was shameful of it all and having never had any real friends to speak of, besides Emily Rose, I didn't want them to think that I was a freak. They were nice to me and invited me to birthday parties. I had never been invited to anyone's birthday party before. It was a foreign world to me. I was ashamed to undress in front of them and when I put on my swimsuit for the hot tub, I was uncomfortable and awkward. I found myself comparing my body to theirs and wished that I was thinner, prettier, and had a better swimsuit. Despite those feelings of self-hatred, the feelings of elation for being there overrode everything else. We talked about boys and making out, things that I instinctively knew were forbidden, but exciting all the same. They were the same things Emily Rose and I had been talking about for a while, but it was different with those girls. They were nice to me and didn't follow every conversation with instruction on how to be prettier and thinner. And though we talked and giggled about those things, it was apparent that they weren't prepared to act on their thoughts.

During the summer I turned eleven, I had a major growth spurt. Suddenly I was five foot six and had breasts. I was uncomfortable with my woman's body, but my new friends didn't seem to notice. We frequented the local skating rink on Friday nights. It was innocent fun and I became quite the speed skater. We would race all the older boys and relished in our triumph when we won. I was lucky enough to have found friends who delighted in music as much as I. We would sing and dance and skate to our hearts content. It was a new escape for me. Friday nights became my most cherished time. A time when I could be free from the reality of life. But as time went on, my grandmother began to question my intentions for going out with my friends. As a young girl, going through puberty, I would often have to deal with the uncomfortable reality of vaginal discharge throughout the day. Back then, panty liners weren't commonly known about and so my underwear wasn't always clean. My grandmother, having no experience with young girls, assumed that the markings were evidence of innocence lost and promptly told my mother that I was making out with boys at the skating rink. I was mortified when my mother brought this up in conversation. Though impure thoughts were a commonality for me, I had never considered acting upon them. And just like that, my grandmother had yet another word to add to her scorn of me. Whore. I was a lazy, selfish, fat, whore. And I honestly had no idea if my mother believed her or not. Worse, I worried that my dad thought those things of me too. I didn't dare ask, but my assumption was that he did. I decided that if he didn't believe those things, he would have been more loving...more present.

My cherished Friday nights became yet another source of stress. I wondered what my family was saying about me after I'd been dropped off. I felt guilt, though I had done nothing wrong. By the end of sixth grade, I had gained a true understanding of what it meant to be depressed. Between the thoughts in my head and the people who had hurt me, I didn't feel safe anywhere I went. I had gone deep inside myself and became a master at wearing a mask. I lived in fear of everything. Mr. Arke. My brothers friend. My Grandmother. My dad. Myself. I wasn't good enough. I wasn't pretty enough. I wasn't skinny enough. I wasn't worthy of love. I lived in pure fear every day. I wanted to escape and often thought about killing myself. Maybe I wasn't brave enough or maybe I still had hope that all the fear would go away. Either way, I could never bring myself to attempt such a final act. I still believed in Prince Charming and knowing what I knew about men, I decided that maybe that was where I would find the love and protection I so desperately needed. My Grandma already thought I was a whore and who knew what Mom and Dad thought.

Words echoed in my head the summer before I began Junior High, like a broken record. Lazy. Ugly. Fat. Whore. All the words that continuously came out of Grandma and Emily Rose's mouths. My parents silence was only confirmation that the words were true. I felt lost and scared, unsure of why I wasn't good enough. I had begun smoking cigarettes because my brother and sister did it and I thought it would make me cool. I locked myself in my room and made myself learn how to inhale. I would have done anything to feel like I belonged somewhere. Even if it only made me feel like I belonged more with my sister. Smoking quickly became my coping mechanism when the stress got to be too much. Which meant I was smoking every day and smoking a lot. My innocence was slowly slipping away; one bad decision after another. But all I heard and all I knew, were the words that echoed in my head.

CHAPTER 5
PUBERTY?

PTSD was not widely understood in the 80's. Christina guided me to the research I needed to understand that the nightmares, the upset stomachs, the depression, peeing my pants, all of it, was my body trying to tell someone, anyone, that something was wrong. But back then, no matter how many times my mother took me to the doctor, it was always the same answer. "She's just going through puberty." And, he was a doctor; I was just a kid. So, my mother believed him and labeled me as a hypochondriac.

****

By the time I entered Junior High, I was consumed by sadness. I was so much older than the kids my age and I found it impossible to relate to them. I had a clear understanding of adult things and I'm certain I wasn't supposed to understand them yet. I had twisted views about sexuality and I honestly believed that if I wasn't offering my body, I would never find love. I was in a hurry to have my first kiss and to lose my virginity. I was becoming more and more boy crazy and yes, part of that was in fact puberty and hormones. I attracted the type of boys who only confirmed my warped beliefs. Still, I clung to the hope that I would someday find my Prince Charming and he would rescue me from all the evil in my life. I believed that my body and my beauty were the key to finding him.

Friday nights at the skating rink continued but the motive changed. I began to notice the high school boys. I was almost fully grown, five foot seven, one hundred twenty pounds, long blond hair, a lean body and a size B cup in the breast. Of course, the boys were noticing me too. I easily passed as fourteen, though I was only twelve. There was something exciting to the notion of lying about my age. The rebellion inside of me was surfacing and I didn't want to stop it. I thought I was a real bad ass. I wore tight jeans, tight tee shirts, long suede boots and suede jackets. I smoked and flirted with any boy who looked my way. The attention was exhilarating, something I had been missing for years. By the end of seventh grade, I was in fact making out with boys in the back of the skating rink and I no longer cared if I was merely confirming my grandmothers' beliefs. The high I got from all the attention was like nothing I had ever felt before. I was beautiful and sexy; just like the women in those magazines I used to peak at.

Emily Rose started spending time with me again once I told her of all the older boys I was meeting. My other friends stopped spending time with me or maybe I stopped spending time with them. Either way, they were no longer a part of my new-found excitement. I made out with various boys, always from schools outside of our district so as not to raise suspicion. If they knew or suspected my real age, they didn't mention it. At school I was still getting straight A's, but outside of school, I was building a reputation. And not one I should have been proud of. But it wasn't anything worse than what I heard at home. At least no one was calling me fat or ugly, just an easy whore. Words that didn't cut when strangers said them. I had reclaimed my Friday nights, the one night where I was in control and could be free of life at home.

I wasn't a stranger to unwanted change, so when my parents announced that we were moving, I wasn't surprised. Moreover, I was angry given the location of our new house. It was a ranch style home, like the one we had lived in when I was little. The house was set on two acres of land, out in the middle of nowhere on a dirt road. Nine miles away from our current home, but too far from civilization for my taste. There was a horse barn and a chicken coop in the back. We already had the horse so that wasn't anything new for me. It was my sisters' horse and I loved him a great deal though I was secretly afraid of him given his size. But chickens...that would take some getting used to. There were only three bedrooms upstairs, but the basement was unfinished. My parents had already planned on remodeling the basement and making two bedrooms, one for me and one for my sister. By this time, we had little to no contact with the Arke's, so I was even unable to find solace in the fact that we were light years away from them. All that mattered to me was that my life was nine miles away and as a teenager, that felt astronomical. I didn't understand what good could come from moving again, but my mother wanted to be able to leave the business at night. She had found her dream home and that was the end of the conversation.

We moved in at the beginning of the summer before my eighth-grade year. My dad advised us of the very strict rules that would accompany our new surroundings. I was only allowed to go in to the family room if invited. I was to spend my time in my room or in the kitchen helping Grandma cook dinner. Everything else upstairs in the house was off limits, unless, of course, I was cleaning. Though, honestly, spending all my time in my room didn't sound like a bad deal. My sister and I were even given our own phone line. Though, the phone was always to stay outside of our rooms. It was a small price to pay for the excitement of having my very own phone number.

My brother had been living on his own for quite some time by then so there was no need to make space for him. In fact, when we moved to the new house, he was living with a woman and was talking about marriage. Her name was Val. My brother had met her when she was pregnant and stuck with her long after. He didn't seem to mind raising another man's child. Val was very nice to me and would ask me to come babysit on the weekends so she and my brother could go out. It was the only time I spent around my brother since he moved out when I was nine. Though they were few and far between, I enjoyed those nights away from Grandma. Babysitting my step-niece allowed a small piece of innocence to return to my heart.

My parents agreed to let me finish out my eighth-grade year at the Junior High I was already in, but I would have to move to the neighborhood High School in ninth grade. My sister got a car that summer and oversaw getting me back and forth. While I was heartbroken over not being with my friends in High School, I was elated that my sister would be my new chauffeur. We listened to loud death metal and smoked like fiends when we were together in the car. I knew I could get away with more if she oversaw driving me because she was more than willing to lie for me. That summer, she let me go to a party with a boy I had met at the skating rink. His name was Devin. Of course, we told my parents that she was simply dropping me off at the skating rink. I knew the party might have meant losing my virginity but with Emily Rose and a couple other promiscuous friends with me, I wasn't afraid. I had just turned thirteen, but the boy thought I was fifteen. The party was at a local teen hang out. The place was overflowing with beer, cigarettes, and hormones. We all met up at Devin's house and then traveled to the party in his friend's van. Devin and I were in the back; my friend Jenna was next to us with a boy she had just met; Emily Rose was in the front with the boy who was driving; and our other friend, Andi, was somewhere in the back of the van, though, I don't remember exactly where. Nothing about the party itself was memorable. It was the ride back home that sticks. Jenna and the boy she had just met were lying next to Devin and me in the back of the van. Devin was trying to get me to have sex with him while Jenna was having sex right next to us. For the first time that night, I was scared and convinced Devin that I was too uncomfortable considering all the people in the back of the van. Angry, he backed off. We didn't speak the rest of the way back to his house and when my sister picked us up, he had already started paying attention to another girl that was with us. We never spoke again. Jenna scolded me for not putting out. Emily Rose simply laughed at me and called me a baby. Andi was too drunk to say anything and ended up puking in the back of my sister's car. Despite the chastising I was getting from my friends, sneaking around and putting myself in danger held an appeal I had not expected.

As I begin my eighth-grade year, the anger inside of me started to swell and played out in every decision I made. I was no longer a straight A student and caring was no longer a part of my MO. I became friends with a few of the stoners and started showing my rebellion at school. Though, I never actually got stoned. Honestly, I didn't fit in with that crowd, but they let me tag along because of Emily Rose. Despite her constant brow beating, I found it easier to spend time with her if it meant I could hang with the cool kids. That's when I met Sam. She too didn't fit in but had been hanging off the coat tails of an old friend who did; just like me. We became fast friends, both of us trying to find our place. We would spend hours listening to 2LiveCrew and reading books. Things just seemed easier with Sam around. She wasn't much into skating but liked the idea of sneaking off to the theater across the street instead. I liked the idea of danger so sneaking around was a perfect fit. We were both boy crazy and anxious to lose our virginity, though, neither one of us were ready. It was an unspoken understanding between us...we talked a good game but when it came time to act, we would chicken out and not a harsh word would be said between us. We met a lot of high school boys at the theater and made out with them on the ledge outside. We never actually saw a movie there, but we always had a good time.

Being at home became more difficult after we moved. My mother's whole reason for moving never came in to play. She was never there. She would head off to work early and get home late in the night. Dad was never there either, though, that was nothing new. Suddenly, I was home alone with Grandma all the time. At least before, my mother was in the same building which offered some sort of comfort. But this new arrangement left me completely stranded with a woman who hated my guts. Given the rules of our movement within the house, I felt that being in my room all the time was what was expected. But this only gave Grandma new material for her complaints. She would tell my parents that I refused to spend time with her, and I would get in trouble constantly for it. I don't remember her ever inviting me to spend time with her, and that was the rule. But it didn't matter what I said. What mattered was that my parents were too busy to deal with Grandma's complaints and I needed to be the one to correct it or be grounded. But fear of Dad and fear of Grandma was a slippery slope that I hadn't quite mastered how to maneuver. If I placed myself upstairs with her when I hadn't been invited, would I get in trouble from Dad? All I felt toward him was fear and that fear overcame everything else that was logical. Suffice it to say, I was grounded a lot. Which meant Sam and Emily Rose were off doing their own things on Friday nights without me.

During the second semester of eighth grade, I met a girl named Loral in Social Studies class. She was new to the school and got seated right next to me. She was the coolest girl I had met in a while and was always nice to me. She was a true stoner and quickly fell in to that crowd. We were loud and disruptive during class, whispering and laughing all the time. The teacher quickly moved her across the room but even that didn't stop us. We passed notes and yelled across the room to each other. Eventually, the teacher would simply kick us out to the hall where we could talk and laugh as much as we wanted without disrupting his class. It felt good to be a bad kid.

During our time in the hall, I noticed numerous cuts on Loral's arms. When I asked her about it, she told me that she did it because it took away the pain. I remember thinking, "Wow, a way to take away the pain? I'm in." She was right. It felt good to inflict the pain on myself. There was a certain high that it gave me, and it took my mind off everything that haunted me. I mainly cut on my arms and sometimes cut on my upper legs. Being that I always had a jacket on, no one noticed. But, by the end of the year, cutting no longer took away the pain as it had in the beginning. So, I turned to something that wasn't obvious. Something that would create wounds that couldn't be seen. Something that would eventually become a dangerous addiction.

By this time, my mother wasn't being as strict as she had been previously, and my groundings were becoming less frequent. I reverted to lying about my Friday night whereabouts. She or my sister would drop me off at the skating rink and my friends and I would run over to the theater. That's when I met Kurt. He had long brown hair and was as skinny as skinny could be. But he was a musician and he was so cool;

a bad boy of sorts. He reminded me of the lead singer from a band I liked at the time. We would make out in front of everyone at the theater or sometimes we would go behind the skating rink if we wanted privacy. I didn't have sex with him, but the high I got from making out with him was noticeable. Something clicked inside my brain and I realized that I had found a way to take away the pain without leaving visible marks on my body.

I moved from boy to boy that summer, eventually ending up in a car with a much older boy who had nothing but sex on his mind. He believed that I was sixteen years old and experienced. We were in the passenger seat and had been making out for a while. He was getting anxious and convinced me to take off my pants. As soon as he tried to enter me, I got scared and pushed him so hard that his back hit his windshield causing it to crack. We didn't have sex, though both he and I told everyone that we did. I thought it would make people think that I was mature and cool if I had already lost my virginity. I also had it in my head that if I told that story, boys would like me more because I was experienced and not some timid little girl. The truth is, I was so scared after that experience that it lessened my desire for the high. I wanted the pain to go away, but I needed to find a different way.

Knowing that I wouldn't be at the same school as my friends the following year, they all but disappeared from my life that summer. I was in the depths of depression and contemplating suicide daily. I wrote dark poetry and withdrew from almost everyone. My parents were rarely home, and I was under Grandma's watch all the time. I hated being home and I hated the idea of going to a school where I knew no one. Sure, I had escaped the monster. But I could never escape my mind and all the horrible tapes it played; repeatedly. I saw Grandma more than I saw my own mother. It was a constant fight and I became a hermit in my room. The more I withdrew, the more time I spent fantasizing about a different life. Every move I made throughout my day was an effort to escape reality.

By the time I started ninth grade, I was angry and unapproachable. I made myself unavailable to new friends and passed quick judgment on anyone who attempted to be nice to me. I dwelled on the fact that I was the new girl and my friends were somewhere else. I spent my nights and weekends attempting to salvage old friendships and refused to make room for new ones. I started dating a guitarist I had met in the school band the year before. He was a nice boy who never once tried to make out with me. He had his problems too though, whatever those were, I didn't know. His name was Luke and he was the quiet type. After my experience in the car with the older boy, I needed someone who was a bit less intense. Emily Rose thought Luke was weird. But I saw something in him. Unfortunately, the distance between us made it hard to have an actual relationship. Sounds funny, as an adult, but as a kid with no car and little means to transportation, nine miles is a lot of distance. By second semester of my ninth-grade year, Luke and I were fighting all the time. We broke up and once again I had no one. I convinced myself to hate my new school and I developed a bad truancy habit. A habit that started a chain of events that would alter my life forever.

CHAPTER 6
RUNAWAY

"It must have made you angry that your Dad wasn't there to protect you." Christina leaned back in her chair. I hadn't even considered that I was angry at him. There were things that happened that he couldn't protect me from due to simple lack of knowledge, and yet, there were things he could have protected me from that were in plain sight. Maybe I wanted him to protect me from all the pain I had experienced in my young life. Or maybe, I had somehow believed that he was supposed to have prevented it from happening in the first place. I was angry with him.

****

I don't remember the exact details that led to my Grandmother moving out of the house when I was fourteen. I know she and my mother had a fight about me. My mom pulled me in to the laundry room one day and told me that I was grounded, but not really. She was fake grounding me to appease my grandmother. I cried hard as a I struggled to understand. I was defeated by the constant brow beating and I couldn't handle it anymore. I was overwhelmed with confusion and caught off guard that my mother was taking my side. It was a bitter sweet moment when Grandma moved out. It meant that I would no longer be her target, but it also meant that I would be home, alone, most of the time. Dad still never came home and in fact, would spend the night at the office even if he wasn't working. I can hardly remember him being in that house when I lived there.

Though Grandma was gone, reality was not. I was more alone; had no friends; and experienced deep pain every day when I woke up. I was ditching most of my classes every day and didn't care about school at all. I stopped going out on Friday nights. Largely because I had lost touch with my friends, and partly because my sister was in college and no longer able to chauffeur me around. When I ditched, I could generally be found in the commons area eating or hanging out in the halls. I would always catch the automated phone call from the school that came in when I got home. Sometimes the machine would answer it, but since Mom never got home until late in the night, I could get it erased and she was none the wiser. I'm sure she received a direct phone call from the school since the ditching didn't stop. Once she found out, I was in a heap of trouble.

She put me on Mom arrest, I couldn't go anywhere except to school without her. She hadn't taken this much interest in me my whole life. I was annoyed and though I was with her, she didn't take the time to find out why I was behaving the way I was. I had been on my own for so long that I couldn't understand what was possibly driving her to care that much. She took me to the office with her one day and we had a fight on the way down. Honestly, I didn't want to fight with her anymore, I just wanted her to be home more. I wanted her to be a part of my life. But, typical to her nature, she was too busy. She sat me down and told me to work on my homework while she finished her work. I'm not sure what made me do it or what I hoped to accomplish. But once she was engrossed in her papers, I took the opportunity and I ran. It wasn't hard to do. I quietly walked out the door and ran down the street. It was cold and foggy. I wasn't dressed to be outside, so I knew I needed to go somewhere close. I wasn't in the mood to deal with Emily Rose and I figured that would be the first place my mother would go.

I ended up at Luke's house. He and I had been talking periodically and were on good terms though we were no longer boyfriend/girlfriend. He was very quiet as he listened to me tell him the story about what had been going on and why I ran away. I don't remember him offering any advice, he just listened, let me cry, and held me. I slept on his floor at night so his Mom wouldn't find me though, I didn't really sleep all that much. He knew he had to get me out of there. I was hungry and I was tired. I was held up in his room for two days and late on the second day, my mom came to their door. Luke's Mom came to his room to ask if he had seen me. Whether she knew he was lying or not, she accepted his answer of "no" and politely told my mother that she would call if they heard from me. After that, I knew I had to leave. Luke quietly snuck me out shortly after my mom left and I walked to Cody's house. Cody was a friend of Emily Rose who had always been kind to me. My mom had just left his house, so he was on high alert. He promised he wouldn't tell but told me I couldn't stay with him. He said he would drive me wherever I wanted to go and that was it. I realized that I needed to find someone to turn to that my mother didn't know. So, I called Jamie, an acquaintance I had made at school.

Jamie was a very kind girl. I met her on the bus at the beginning of the year. We were the only two who got off at that stop and she was always nice to me. She welcomed me in to her house with open arms and promised that her and her mom would help me. Unbeknown to me, her mom was a social worker. I told Jamie small bits about my grandmother and my dad. But I did tell her one lie. One lie that would change everything. I have a scar on my knee. I have no idea how I got that scar. But I told Jamie that it was from my dad. Though my dad was very loud and scary, he hadn't hit me since right before Grandma moved out. On one rare occasion, he had come home late in the evening. She lied to him and told him that I refused to eat dinner with her. That night I was reminded of why I feared him so much. I woke up to him pushing open my door and screaming at me. He dragged me up the stairs by my hair and shoved my head in to the microwave. I was confused because I didn't know dinner was ready. I had fallen asleep and if Grandma indeed had called for me, I didn't hear her. I only woke when my dad turned on my light and started screaming. But I didn't tell Jamie that story. I told her a lie about my knee because that was a mark and I thought a mark would mean that she would believe me. I didn't have any marks left from the microwave incident. Not visible anyway; just an extra year with my braces and a lie to the Orthodontist that I had been in a fight. Jamie's mom agreed to let me stay the night, but only if I turned myself in to the school counselor the next day. And that is what we did.

The counselor reported my dad to social services. I remember him sitting in her office yelling at me and at one point he leaned forward as if he were going to strike me. I'm sure that only confirmed for the counselor the story I had told. Whether I lied or not, the truth was, my fear of Dad was evident and pure. And though he didn't hit often, he did hit and grab and push on occasion. When we first moved in to that house, he got angry with me because I didn't get all the dog poop picked up. He yelled and screamed at me and grabbed my arm hard. He was so angry, and I didn't understand why. The grass was tall, and I was not the one in charge of mowing. There was no way I could have seen the dog poop where it was, but that didn't matter. When he was angry, all logic was set aside and there was no defending myself. When we were finally allowed to leave the school, my dad was so angry that he refused to look at me. He declared that he was moving out. My mom was furious. She said that I could ruin their business by doing what I had done. My dad worked closely with the local police departments and he could lose his contracts because of my allegations. We would lose our house and everything they had worked so hard for. She made sure that I had a clear understanding that it was all because of me. All I wanted was for him to be the dad that played and wrestled on the floor. I didn't want him to yell or hit anymore. I didn't want him to be mad all the time. I just wanted him to be my dad again. I couldn't bear to be the reason my parents' business was destroyed. I wanted normal. The normal I had when I was four years old, sitting on my sisters' bicycle on the back porch; the back covered porch of our cookie cutter home. After hours of listening to my mother yell at me and ridicule me, I agreed to tell the social worker that it was all a lie. Every bit of it. They dropped the charges, but my dad didn't come home. He bought a condo close to the office and wrote me out of his life. Not that it was any different than the way things were before he moved out. He hadn't been a part of my life for years. What made this different was that he verbalized that he no longer wanted me in his life. That made it real...more hurtful. At least before it was because he was working, not because he hated me.

With my sister two hundred miles away at college, I didn't have anyone to turn to. It was just me and my mom for the rest of the school year and she wasn't speaking to me much. And since she was always at work, it quickly became, just me. My depression got worse and I was constantly contemplating suicide. I didn't know how I would do it. I just knew that I wanted to. I was completely alone and had no one, not even friends, to talk to about my home life. Luke and I stopped talking; Emily Rose was so self-absorbed that talking to her about anything was pointless; Sam, Lorel, and Jamie weren't exactly people I felt comfortable crying to. I hadn't befriended anyone else at the new school and there were no other family members that I was close to. I felt sad and afraid all the time. Only now, I was afraid of different things. Afraid of my mom leaving me too. Afraid of not having anyone to love me. Afraid of telling anyone the truth about anything in my life.

I began living in my fantasy world. My mother moved my room upstairs in case I tried to run away again. She grounded me for the entire summer. My sister came back from college and though that helped a little, it didn't make the pain disappear. I was happy to have my best friend back. She was the only one who believed in me and the only one who loved me, no matter what. But she was still a teenager too and had her own life to live. She couldn't offer me the help I needed, only a shoulder to cry on.

I quickly found ways around my grounding. For some reason, my mother didn't include my sister or my cousin in my groundings. Probably not a wise move on her part. My cousin and I went to the local amusement park one day and met a couple of random college boys. We convinced them that we too were in college and exchanged numbers. The attention the boys gave us occupied my mind and gave me a moment of relief from all the pain. It was a high I had experienced before but shied away from out of fear. One of the boys called me the next day and asked to come over while my mom was at work. I told him yes and he showed up, wanting nothing but sex. I had just turned fifteen, was still a virgin, and was on my period. I told him that it was my time of the month and he didn't care. He pushed me up against the wall and kept ordering me to "take it out" over and over. I refused to comply with his demands and kept asking him to stop. He had me pinned up against the wall and kept kissing my neck. I think he thought I was turned on, but I was scared to death and mad for getting myself in to that situation. I started to push back, and he eventually let go of me and stormed out of the house.

I locked all the doors and hid in my room for the rest of the day. I didn't understand why I got myself in to precarious situations such as these. But even more, I didn't understand why I got a high out of him wanting me like that. Fear would peak just enough to kill the high and stop the act, but the high...it took away all the pain. It made everything disappear. I knew I was playing with fire. I didn't want to, but I didn't want to stop either. I needed to find a different way to numb the pain.

CHAPTER 7
REHAB

"Why didn't you tell your therapist the truth when you were in the rehabilitation center?" Christina had that look on her face that told me she knew the answer but was asking anyway. Fear. Pure, unadulterated fear. If I told the truth, I would be punished. It was easier to pretend that everything was okay than risk losing more than I already had.

****

At the start of my sophomore year, my mom agreed to give me a fresh start. I was relieved to have my freedom back, even though I didn't really have anyone to hang out with. I decided that I would attempt to make a couple of friends or at least talk to people in class. It paid off. I made a friend named Jenny. She was a Freshman, but she was so much like me. She had an attitude and was the perfect amount of rebellious. We became fast friends and starting ditching classes together. I was beginning the same pattern as the year before but this time, I had an accomplice. We were careful not to ditch the same classes more than once per week. That seemed to ward off the

Dean.

By the time Homecoming came around, my mom still hadn't caught wind that I was ditching again. She allowed me to attend the dance with my new friend Jenny. That's the night I met Jacob Dean. We were put together by a mutual acquaintance of ours, Kyle. Kyle was always in trouble and always trying to get in my pants. That night was no different. I'm certain it was not his intention to put Jacob and I together, but to avoid the school security officer, he asked Jacob to dance with me until he got back. He never came back. Jacob was different than the boys I usually fell for. He was six foot three, slender, clean cut and had beautiful baby blue eyes. He wore a dorky purple suit and I remember distinctively when Jenny expressed her distaste for him. We danced for a bit but at the end of the night, we went our separate ways without exchanging numbers. I didn't think much about him the rest of the weekend. He was a Senior and I was a Sophomore so I figured he wouldn't give me a second thought.

The following Monday morning, during passing period, a girl from my class tracked me down and informed me that she had a friend whose brother wouldn't stop talking about me all weekend. I knew of his sister, Jayell, because we were in the same grade, though I didn't have any classes with her. She was very smart and in all the hard classes. But, by the end of that day, we had embarked on a friendship that I would come to cherish more than I could have ever expected. After school, she shuffled me down the hallway to reintroduce me to her brother, Jacob Dean. I wasn't expecting anything to come of it, but I figured it wouldn't hurt to try. I remember thinking that it sure would be nice to make some new friends at that school. And by the end of the week, Jacob, Jayell and I were all becoming close. For the first time in years, I felt like I belonged.

Jacob was different from other boys. He wasn't

shallow, he listened to me when I spoke, and he didn't want me to throw myself at him. It was weird. Being so far outside of my element made it difficult to adjust my behaviors. I continuously threw myself at him. The first two weeks we hung out after school were filled with making out and small talk. The making out was due to my advances and the small talk was due to his desire to get to know me. He was good and his motives were pure. He wanted an actual relationship, one where sex would simply be a pleasant benefit. Jayell and I began hanging out during passing periods and lunch. She too was good and pure. It felt odd to me, having people in my life like them. Jenny didn't approve and made sure to voice her opinion each day in class. But I was intrigued. I wanted to know them both. It felt right and it felt good.

But my life was still my life and in keeping up with patterns, the end of those first two weeks held yet another change. It was a Friday, and I was excited for the weekend because Jacob and I had plans. My mom came home from work early...something that simply never happened. She had a funny look on her face as she told me that we were going out for ice cream. After about twenty minutes in the car, I realized that we were not, in fact, going to Dairy Queen. We traveled along the highway, and I knew that something scary was about to happen. The sun set and by the time we reached our destination, it was dark. I had been there before, a few times after my dad moved out. They said I needed therapy because of the lies I told and that was where my therapist's office was. It was also a rehabilitation center that sat on a hill in the outskirts of our city. The parking lot was dark when we arrived, allowing the yellow lights inside the building to shine bright through each window. It's hard to describe the way it felt as we pulled up; I was afraid, I was angry, and a voice inside my head told me that it was the end. I knew we were there for more than just an appointment, but I didn't dare voice my suspicions.

My mother took me inside to the office of my therapist. They explained to me that they were admitting me in to the rehabilitation center for inpatient care. I thought the idea was ludicrous. I was not an addict and thought that was what those places were for. They told me that my emotional problems were so bad that this was the only way. I had been diagnosed with Severe Manic Depression and my mom said I was completely out of control. Obviously, she had discovered that I was ditching again. I fought hard at first. I cried and begged my mom to give me one more chance. It wasn't until I saw the big scary guy outside the door with a gurney and restraints that I settled down and accepted my fate. I listened quietly as they took me through the intake process. When that was complete, a nurse came and lead me to a part of the building I hadn't been in yet. There was a security door with long windows that led to a nurse's station and what looked to be a living room. As the door closed heavy behind me, I turned around and saw my mom walking out of the doctor's office. I could only glare at her with nothing but pure hatred in my heart.

The nurse took me to a bedroom and explained that I would be sharing it with another girl who had been there for a while. On the bed was a bag that my mother must have packed for me while I was at school that day. The nurse told me to strip down naked and advised that she would need to search me. I was humiliated and wondered if this was how a criminal felt. I knew she was just doing her job; there was no way she could have known that strip searching me would bring up so many feelings of shame and worthlessness. But I hated her anyway. After the search, I was instructed to take a three-minute shower. As if they wanted me to wash the bad off. The nurse stood outside the bathroom door the whole time I was in there. When I was done, she told me to get dressed and probably other instructions too, though, I don't remember them. After I was dressed, I sat on the bed and looked around the room. There were two twin size beds, two night stands, two dressers, a lamp, and a small window with bars on it. I'm not sure how long I had been sitting there when I realized that my shoes were gone. Somehow, not having my shoes made me realize the reality of the situation. I lay down on the bed and cried for what seemed like hours. I stared at the ceiling and wondered why I was being punished for all the pain I had experienced in my life. It seemed unjust. Anger stifled my tears and I fell asleep, determined to find a way out of the rehab.

I met my roommate early the next morning. I wish I could tell you that I remember her name, but I don't. She was a very kind and friendly girl who was there for drug addiction. I immediately thought myself unworthy of being there considering my issues weren't chemical. But she didn't seem to care and quickly went over the lay of the land with me. She explained that if they took my shoes, that meant they thought I was a run risk. We laughed because the security in that place would make it almost impossible to run. She stuck with me the entire day; helping me figure out the schedule and understand the rules. I learned that I would not be allowed to have my shoes for forty-eight hours and that I could earn phone time for good behavior. Behavior was based off your participation in the program. The more you participated, the more points you earned. The more points you earned, the more privileges you earned. It was a very simple system, one that I was certain I could master. She introduced me to all the kids on the floor. There were about seven of us and only one other girl was there for mental issues. Everyone else was there due to a chemical dependency. The other girl like me wasn't social at all and was clearly in a bad head space. I wondered if my mother would think differently of my mental stability had she met that girl. But overall, everyone there was kind and accepting of me.

The day schedule was easy enough to follow. We had chores to be done every morning before breakfast, then we attended "school", and then we had both individual therapy and group therapy. The evening schedule was a bit more intimidating. We had family group therapy once a week; this was where everyone's family came in and we all sat in one big group together. That was awkward most of the time. My dad came once but that was it. Then there was Alcoholics Anonymous twice a week. I had the choice between Alcohol or Narcotics. I chose alcohol probably because I had actually drank once before. Still, I was very uncomfortable, and it was clear that I did not belong in that group. But I was determined to earn phone privileges, so I conformed to all the rules with a smile on my face. I earned my shoes back by Sunday night. I earned phone privileges by the following Wednesday. By the end of week one, they moved me from inpatient to outpatient because I wasn't presenting enough mental issues to show a need for twenty four-hour care. My compliance and positive attitude were working in my favor.

Upon hearing the news that I was leaving the inpatient program, my roommate instructed me on how to sneak in cigarettes. It was simple, put the cigarettes under my bra, in between my breasts. It was an area that wasn't checked on outpatient participants. I happily obliged because being bad felt pretty good. And being their cigarette supplier made me even more popular. It made being there more bearable. Everyone in the program, including the adults, would question why I was there. I didn't seem as messed up as the other kids were and my positive attitude about my situation seemed odd to them. Pretending to be someone I was not had become common place for me over the years, so it came easily. I pretended that there was nothing wrong with me and put on my best face for everyone there. Even my caseworker questioned my need for the program. In therapy, whether it was group or individual, I focused on easy to solve problems like ditching and getting bad grades. I didn't even scratch the surface of the pain that kept me up at night. I was determined to get back to my life; to get back to the boy. By the end of week two, I had convinced all the adults at the facility that there was no need for me to be there every day and just as fast I was admitted, I was released.

They threw me a goodbye party, and everyone wrote me messages in a "Goodbye Book". The most common theme of the book was how quickly I got out and that no one could believe that I had healed so fast. At the time, I wasn't interested in healing. I had one focus and one focus only...Jacob Dean. He was what took away the pain and I didn't believe that anything else could.

CHAPTER 8
PRINCE CHARMING

Christina taught me to visualize a safe space that makes me feel at peace. It brought back a memory from my high school years which prompted me to find a poem I wrote back then...

The light of the stars comforts me in the darkness. I am stronger at night, when the others are at rest. No one can hurt me here. Though I am alone, I am safe from their words, their hands, and their deception. My focus becomes how to escape the harm that it is being done to me. While I don't quite understand the depth of my wounds, it is clear that they are there, and they must be healed. My young mind tells me that running is the answer. My wise mind tells me the wounds will not disappear if I am gone. I lay awake, confused by the day and unsure of what my next action should be. There is nowhere to run; nowhere to hide; and nowhere safe. I finally fall asleep fantasizing about the day my prince charming will come and rescue me from this hell. One day, he will make it all disappear.

****

Jacob Dean was my Prince Charming. When I was released from Rehab, we quickly reconnected. He wasn't upset with me for my abrupt absence. He didn't judge me when I told him the story of why my mom sent me away. All my insecurities and self-perceptions were meaningless to him. He liked me because I was me and he wanted to be with me. That's all it took for me to fall; and fall hard. But I didn't just fall for Jacob Dean. Jayell was quickly becoming my new best friend. She was a refreshing change from Emily Rose. Her intelligence astounded me. I sometimes wondered if she really was as smart as she seemed considering she was hanging out with someone like me. But my past and my style didn't seem to faze her. She was much like her brother, and only cared about the person I showed her, not the person I had been.

Jacob Dean was a respectful, polite, and kind young man. He never pressured me, and he never made me feel worthless. In fact, I knew I could tell him anything and he would still want to be with me. But even that wasn't enough to prevent me from lying to him. I don't know why I lied; I just did. Even though he was never pushy, I still believed that he wouldn't want me if he knew I was a virgin. He himself was not and he had been honest with me about his previous relationship. But I could not bring myself to be honest with him; to tell him that I was a virgin and was simply putting on an act thinking that it would make him like me more. Maybe it would have changed everything; maybe it would have changed nothing. By not telling him the truth, I robbed myself of something. I had no one to share my first with; I couldn't even share it with him. He was one of the only men who did not expect me to put out within the first few days of our relationship. At the time, that was foreign to me. I thought it meant that there was something wrong with me. But Jacob Dean didn't seem to think that. And when we did finally sleep together, he was kind, attentive, and very concerned with my wellbeing. I knew that he was exactly what I needed.

Despite the views I held of sex and love, I wanted the fairy tale. I wanted to believe that men were not evil, and that true love did exist. I wanted, what I believed to be, the perfect love story; meet the love of your life in high school, get married, have kids, live happily ever after. I put all the pressure of turning that dream into a reality on Jacob. And at first, he was able to deliver. We had a lot of fun together. We would hang out after school and eat everything in his house or mine. His mother was amazing and turned out to be a great influence in my life. In fact, I believe that if it weren't for her, I would not have survived my teen years. She replaced the vacancy of my mother when I needed her the most. I had never known love the way Jacob's family gave it. They didn't care that I had a rough past and was riddled with mental problems. They loved me for the person I was, not the pain I was suffering. Jacob and I would watch television, or he would help me with my homework; that was the only year I got good grades in high school. We would go for drives with the radio cranked up and just be kids. It was like nothing I had ever known before. Some days it didn't feel real. But when Jacob took my hand in the morning, my heart skipped a beat and I was reminded of my new reality. I was completely immersed in him and his family and never wanted to leave. They showed me what healthy love looked like. It was the fairytale slowly coming to life.

Jacob was not without his faults and our relationship slowly became one of rage and violence. The combination of my insecurities and his anger issues brought out the worst in both of us. Within a few months of our love story, we were fighting a lot. My fear that he would leave brought about unwarranted accusations and irrational thinking. If he didn't want to have sex with me, I would immediately think that he didn't love me anymore. His reaction was less than favorable.

He was rough and would often hurt me. I can't say that he ever actually hit me, but I do recall a couple of times when either my sister or his would step in and tell him to stop hurting me. But I don't remember how he was hurting me; I simply remember that he did. Though, I believe he never did it intentionally. Not to say that I excuse his actions, simply to say, he had a past too and his was one full of violence. Together, we were a toxic mix. Depression started to take over me again and Jacob was trying desperately to pull me out of it. I didn't understand how something, seemingly so perfect, could hurt so much. By Prom, we were miserable. I had become the classic psycho girlfriend; controlling and needy. Every step he made was wrong and every interaction held negative connotation. I was a mess and I was making him a mess too.

As the classic great love stories go, ours came to an end very shortly after he graduated high school. We tried for a few weeks to see if we could repair the relationship, but it was clear that his heart wasn't in it. I was devastated. Unable to see my part in the breakup, I took it as yet another rejection from a person I loved. What made it harder was that his sister had become my best friend, in fact, she was my only real friend by that point. His mother had replaced my mother. I didn't know if I would lose all of them or just him. But their ability to love proved true when Jayell and Mom promised me that they would not severe our relationships. It was bittersweet. Being around them was a constant reminder of Jacob. But I needed them more than I needed him. I had no one else to help me find my way once he was gone.

It took me years to get over Jacob Dean. For the month after our breakup, I begged and pleaded for him to come back to me. It was quite pathetic. After repeatedly turning me down, I went in to a deep depression. I was completely lost and unable to cope. I had spent so much time building him up and making him my all that I never once stopped to consider the "what ifs". I was unprepared and didn't bother to learn any tools at rehab that would help me through such a difficult time. In my mind, his leaving was confirmation that I was bad and unworthy of love. He was just another person who abandon me because I was me. This likely pushed me toward Jayell more. She was the only person who seemed to understand what I was feeling, and she rarely left my side.

The devastating pain hit me square in the chest every day I woke up. Day after day. I was lost without him and didn't know how I could possibly go on. I had made him my everything and my everything was gone. When we were together, it felt like he took away the pain and the reality of my family life. I placed all my faith in him. Without him, life went back to the way it was. My dad was gone; my mom was always gone; my sister was off on her own - living her own life. And I... was alone. I no longer had the distraction. That person who made everything else seem non-existent. He was gone and he had taken the most important piece of me with him; hope.

By my sixteenth birthday, I was in the darkest place I had ever been. It was supposed to be the best day ever. At least, that is what I had told myself for years. I didn't get the "sweet sixteen" that everyone always talked about. While my brother and sister got cars when they turned sixteen, I did not. If I wanted a car, I would have to pay for it myself. Another reminder that I was the bad kid, undeserving of anything due to the turmoil I had caused. My mom did let me throw a party the weekend before my actual birthday. There were a lot of people there, including Jayell and her new boyfriend that I didn't like. Most of the kids that were there were my sisters' friends and of course, Emily Rose. But it didn't bring me out of the state of mind I was in. There was no car, no Jacob, and no dad. I was lost and completely alone. I wished that they would all just leave. The only person I wanted there was Jacob

Dean.

My actual birthday landed on the Wednesday after my party. It was like any other day and there was still no car in the driveway when I woke up. I'm not sure why I clung to that dream for so long, but I did. Mom went to work, and I was left home alone to tend to my chores. It was a very lonely day. None of my friends called; Jacob didn't call; and there was no confetti or ribbons of any kind. Just a typical day. Evening came, but my mom did not. She was working late or something. Being alone gave me time to think about the horrible person I was and how much of a disappointment I was to the people I loved. I reflected on all the events that occurred in my life. Mr. Arke, my brothers' friend, my grandmother, my dad, mean kids at school, Emily Rose, Jacob...all of it. I determined that the common denominator was me. I resolved that the world would be better off without me. It's not that I wanted to die as much as it was that I wanted the pain to end. So, on my Sixteenth Birthday, alone in a five-bedroom house, I took a bottle of prescription pills from the medicine cabinet and a bottle of vodka from the pantry. I downed them both.

Much to my disappointment, I awoke in the middle of the night to see my mother coming into the house in what appeared to be a drunken state. My dad was with her, helping her to the bedroom. I was on the couch, alive, but sick as the dickens. I was sick for days after, throwing up repeatedly and in so much pain I could hardly stand. I didn't dare tell anyone what I had done for fear that I would get thrown back in to the rehab center again. I forced myself to push through the pain and the vomiting. I likely should have had my stomach pumped, but by the grace of a higher power, I made it through, alive.

I made myself a promise after that night. I promised that I would never allow anyone or anything in my life to let me get that low again. I knew that I survived for a reason and for a moment, I believed in a higher power and that he, or she, was carrying me through the pain. Though I didn't understand why the pain had been allowed to occur in the first place. Something I would not understand or even attempt to investigate until much later in life. All I knew was that I was clearly supposed to be here. But, as any logical minded teenager would do, I determined that this was a sign from the higher ups that I was supposed to live my life doing what made me happy, regardless of the consequences. I thought that I had hit rock bottom and bounced back up. Little did I know, this was only the beginning of my downward spiral. A spiral that would grossly impact not only me, but anyone else who crossed my path for the next twenty years of my life.

PART TWO

A DANGEROUS ADDICTION

"One thing you must realize is that: you either kill your addiction, or your addiction will eventually kill you." ~ *Oche Otorkpa*

CHAPTER 9
ADDICTION

"It's very common for women who are sexually abused as children to become promiscuous when they get older." Christina announced. By this stage of my therapy I felt that I could trust her whole heartedly, but I still went home and researched her statement. You would have thought that it provided me relief to know that my self-destructive actions were in fact a result of the things that were done to me as a child. But it didn't. I still felt deep shame and guilt. I'm not sure if anyone ever really recovers from that.

****

Even though I never told Jayell about my suicide attempt, she seemed to instinctively know that I needed her. We spent most of our time together that summer. I bought myself an old car and got a job working at a local restaurant. We hung out at the mall and met a boy named Eddie. His name wasn't Eddie, but he was from the Middle East and his name was difficult to pronounce. He chose the name Eddie because it seemed to be a name Americans could say. He was kind and respectful though it was often difficult to understand him when he spoke. He was the only boy I dated after Jacob that I didn't have sex with. We would sit on my couch and watch television, but he wouldn't dare act on my advances. I mistook his respect for rejection and quickly determined that he wasn't worth my while. I needed to feel wanted because that was the only way I knew how to feel love. I stopped seeing him very shortly after we started dating and never heard from him again. My depression continued to build and even Jayell couldn't keep me from feeling lost.

By the time I entered my Junior Year of High School, I was a ticking time bomb. The feelings of wanting to run became more and more overwhelming. But I knew I couldn't run, and risk being put back in rehab. I had to get away without running away. Jayell and her mom stood by my side and did their best to help me through. But being with them only made it more difficult. They were a constant reminder of Jacob. Yet, I wasn't willing to lose their friendship. So, I figured out how to run without running. It was a dangerous line and I had found a way to walk it. I reconnected with the boy who had introduced me to Jacob in the first place, Kyle. I knew he was trouble and that all he wanted was sex. But suddenly, I didn't care. I quickly discovered that meaningless sex numbed the pain that had become a part of my identity. During our time in the bedroom my head would clear, the world would disappear, and the pain was gone. I would feel guilt and shame after every time we were together, but I wasn't willing to give up those brief moments of relief. I found myself unable to think of anything else and I was constantly wanting more. Sex became my drug, my addiction. So, when Kyle moved on, I shrugged him off and moved on too.

Though I thought of Jacob often, my new addiction made it easy to occupy my mind. I convinced myself that younger guys were not the answer; that they were too immature to know how to take care of a girl like me. I began looking to older boys, in their early twenties, for confirmation of my logic. That's when I met Evan Jones. He wasn't anything special. He was five-foot seven blondish hair, freckles, skinny, wore glasses. I don't even remember the color of his eyes. I just remember that he was older than me, twenty-four, and he paid attention to me. We met at the restaurant I worked at. He was a cook. I was a bus girl. I came around the corner one night and he yelled, "Oooh Ieesha!". He thought I was so cute. I thought he was such a dork. The man I really had my sights on was Markus Stone. He was also a cook and older. But he wouldn't give me the time of day and Evan, he paid attention. Everyone told me that he was married. But when I confronted Evan about it, he told me he was separated, and they were getting a divorce. My self-esteem was non-existent, and my naivety was high. I wanted to believe that what Evan was telling me was true. So, I did.

Our relationship started out as nothing more than sex. He wanted anyone who wasn't his wife and I wanted to get high. But spending time together meant getting to know each other. That meant developing feelings for each other. Which led to relationship status and drama. He was always trying to hide his lies from me, and I quickly became suspicious of him. But I couldn't bring myself to walk away. He was my first real hardcore drug and I couldn't focus on much more than satisfying my cravings.

Within a month of our seeing each other, Evan left the restaurant and went to work for a rental company. It was then that my thoughts started to fill with shame, guilt, and worthlessness almost immediately following every encounter. Those feelings only got worse as I continued to compromise myself and he began to want more excitement. He came to my house in his new delivery truck one day. He begged me to come

77

outside and have sex with him in the back of the truck. The thought clearly excited him and even though I was incredibly uncomfortable with the idea, I followed him. Regardless of how it made me feel about myself, I couldn't turn down the opportunity to be numb. Even though I knew that what I was doing wasn't right, I couldn't stop. He left immediately following our adventure and I walked back inside the house with my head hung low and my body trembling.

Shortly after that encounter, I was diagnosed with an STD. I was mortified and humiliated. The only way to cure it was through surgery. The day of the surgery I felt like everyone at the hospital was judging me and calling me a whore. I'm sure they weren't, but I was. That night, Evan came over and even though the doctor told me I couldn't have sex for weeks, Evan persisted. The moment he began to enter me, I knew that it was a bad idea and begged him to stop, but he wouldn't. I bit my lip to stop myself from screaming in pain while tears flowed from my eyes. It seemed like forever before he was finally done and when he was, he looked me in the eyes and told me he loved me. I should have been angry, I should have kicked him out, I should have done something. But when he said those three little words, I did nothing.

He moved out of his marital home in to an apartment right after. That's when things started to change. I found myself unable to get the same high from him as I did before. He had given me a key to his apartment, and we started playing house. The sex was no longer satisfying, and he started to get angry about it. We began frequently engaging in physical fights when I realized that he was in fact still seeing his wife. I wanted to believe that he loved me, but I knew that he didn't. I wanted to love him, but I knew I didn't. Our toxic relationship quickly became poisonous and we parted ways.

Jayell and I were starting to grow apart as well. Partly because I was out of control and partly because her boyfriend and I did not get along. My grades at school had dropped again and I wasn't interested in making new friends. My only focus was getting high. And though I was sad about breaking up with Evan Jones, he was easy to forget once Markus Stone turned his attention to me. After all, he was the man I had originally been pining for. Maybe it was his motorcycle; maybe it was because he was so much older than I; or maybe it was those stark blue bedroom eyes that caused me to melt every time I saw him. Whatever it was, that man had my attention. He was everything I knew to be sexy. Five foot nine, slim yet muscular build, tidy brown hair and those eyes. Forever engraved in my brain are those baby blues. He could hold my attention and convince me to do anything with those eyes. I was head over heels in lust with him from the moment I met him. He was twenty-three and I was sixteen. I had been on a quest to find a new dealer since Evan and I broke up, one who could offer an even better drug. Boy did Markus deliver.

At first, he was hesitant to involve himself with me because of our age difference. Still, he was paying attention and testing the waters. And given my newly developed ability to manipulate, compliments of Evan Jones, I was able to wear Markus down quickly. I had, what I thought, become a master in the ways of men, knowing that sex held a power even I didn't understand. Age had become a minor detail when I caught Markus Stone.

The first night we went out, he took me on his motorcycle. I had never ridden one before and I was immediately hooked. We sped down a deserted road while my arms were locked tight around his body. The freedom I felt was exhilarating and the fear of it all was a turn on. I knew being with him would be dangerous. I knew he was someone I could easily fall for. But I dove in anyway, desperate for the high. His ex-girlfriend was still living in his apartment at the time. She was my first experience with the term "psycho-ex".

We would go to an open field to hang out and party with friends. We lovingly referred to it as "the fields". The property was owned by a friend of Markus' who happened to also be a friend of my friend Cody. I'll never forget the night that I ran over a mile in sandals, through wet grass and gravel, to escape the psycho ex. We generally hung out and partied in the middle of the fields. We were all out there, drinking beer and having fun when she arrived. The guys told me to run and hide behind the porta potties while they convinced her to leave. She was there specifically looking for me, the home-wrecker. Though, honestly, I didn't realize that I was one at the time. Once they got her to her car, Cody's girlfriend came back to me and told me where I needed to meet them and that they would take me home. By this age, I was no longer an athletic girl. But when she told me to run, I ran...over a mile, through wet grass and gravel, in a pair of strappy white sandals with literally no soles. By the time I reached Cody's car, my calves were cramped, and I could hardly walk. When they dropped me off at home, the cramps were so bad that I could only crawl to the back door of my house. There I sat, on the back steps, laughing so hard I was crying. I couldn't even stand to open the door. My mother was inside on the phone; I was late for curfew. She simply looked at me with a funny look, opened the door, and continued her conversation. In hind sight, I suppose her indifference to my existence at that moment was a good thing. I don't know how I could have explained the events of the evening without divulging information that might upset her.

The fun Markus and I had lasted all spring and in to the summer. After his ex-girlfriend moved out, we didn't waste any time getting to the bedroom. As I had suspected, he was able to numb my pain longer than anyone else before him. I couldn't get enough and wanted to be with him every second of the day. We would hang out for hours, watch television, talk about nothing, and laugh together. He eventually quit the restaurant we worked at and started working at a little hole in the wall grill, across town. I would go to eat dinner there while he was working. Markus and I would flirt with each other endlessly until his shift was over and we could go for a ride on his bike. It was the ultimate foreplay. He had a way of making me feel high as a kite, regardless of what we were doing.

I wanted him to be the one that could take Jacob and Dad's place. The one that could satisfy my addiction for good. I tried to make him settle down and commit to me. But he just wasn't that kind of man. He wanted to come home from work, drink a lot of beer, and veg out in front of the television. He didn't want to tell me about his life. In fact, I couldn't even begin to tell you anything about his childhood, his parents, or anything like that. He was a mystery. I suppose that was some of his appeal. Our age difference continued to be a topic of conversation and added strain to our relationship. Our time together started to get mundane and I wanted more from him than he was willing to give. He was always buzzed from the beer by the time we got in to bed, but it didn't matter to me. He was satisfying my addiction and bringing back my ability to experience hope. Of course, I also thought it was cool that my boyfriend could buy beer and drink it legally. I started to get clingy and difficult when he refused to commit to me the way I wanted him to. The harder I pushed, the harder he pushed back. Eventually, he broke things off citing our age difference as something he could no longer handle. I suppose that was true to a degree. I think he recognized that I was addicted, he was my drug, and he couldn't handle that.

By this time, Jayell and I were no longer spending time together. She had her boyfriend and he made it clear that he had no want for me to be around. I told myself that it was for the best. Her and her mother's loyalty needed to be to Jacob, not to me. Though I missed her a great deal, I didn't tell her. I was consumed with trying to find the feeling that Markus gave me when we were together. It seemed to be all that mattered at the time.

Markus didn't disappear from my life completely after that. He eventually became my go to when I needed the high-quality drug only he seemed to be able to deliver. He would numb my pain and I would leave. Secretly, I wanted him to tell me that he loved me and that he wanted to be everything I needed him to be. That would eventually happen, but only when it was too late.

The last time I went to Markus he broke my heart and I developed an immunity to his drug. He had moved to a small house in the heart of the city. I was looking for more than sex that night. But not Markus. I had set a precedent and he had come to accept that that was all our relationship was. There was no conversation. He led me straight to his bed and when we were done, led me straight back to the door to leave. I had never felt so cheap in my life. He may as well have paid me as he pushed me out the door. I vowed never to see him again.

I heard from him once, many years after that. It was Christmas and I was pregnant with my oldest son. My mom took me back to her room and pulled out an envelope. As she handed it to me, she advised that it was left on their front door sometime in the night. It was a note from Markus. He realized that he and I always seemed to find each other. He wanted to try an actual relationship and asked me to call him. I told my mother to throw the note away and we went about our Christmas business. I haven't heard from Markus Stone since.

CHAPTER 10
THE ONE WHO GOT AWAY

"Do you think you need closure on those relationships?"
Christina had a look of genuine concern on her face. I suppose
we all feel a need for closure on relationships that go bad. But
at this stage in my life, why open Pandora's Box? They all
moved on and so have I. There is nothing I could say or do
that would change what happened. I sit with the pain and work
hard to forgive myself. Closure won't change the outcome.

****

Markus and I broke up early in the summer before my senior
year of high school. I had quit the restaurant and was working
for a Private Investigator who rented office space at my
parents' business. Since Jayell and I had stopped talking, I
found myself spending more time with my sister and her
friends. It helped pass the time but being away from Markus
was like having withdrawals. I cried a lot; over him, over Jacob,
over me. I wasn't exactly sure what I was mourning but I was

in pain and needed something to numb it. Looking for a quick high, I reached out to Kyle again. By this time, he was engaged, and his fiancé was pregnant. But Kyle, being the excellent dealer he was, understood exactly what I needed and immediately introduced me to a couple of guys in the complex he lived in. They were brothers, living on their own in the ultimate bachelor pad. There was no furniture in the front room; just a mattress on the floor. I didn't care about that; I was looking for a high and Kyle promised that at least one of them would deliver. The youngest of the two was only a year older than I. The older was in his mid-twenties. Keeping with my theory that older men were better, I sought him out first. He wasn't good looking, but he wasn't ugly. The sex was boring and didn't offer me the satisfaction I was craving. I had become so reliant on the high-quality drug of Markus Stone that my expectations were beyond reach. Out of boredom and the need for more, I moved on to the younger brother. I knew what I was doing was wrong; I had become a whore and all that mattered to me was finding the right drug to numb my pain. At the time, I needed the high more than I needed to be a better person.

Though short lived, the younger brother satisfied my addiction better than the older one. It quickly became an argument between the two and I wasn't interested in being part of their drama even though I was the source of it. They had a neighbor, a much older man in his late thirties. He was handsome and suave; it was clear that he knew how to play a woman. He was a smooth talker and quickly convinced me that I needed a real man; not these boys who couldn't satisfy me and wouldn't stop fighting over me. It was easy for him to get me in his bed. He was well endowed and though some women might find that appealing, I was not a woman. I was a girl and that was not the drug for me. Our one encounter was awkward and painful. I never saw him again after that. In fact, I never saw any of them again after that.

There were a couple more random men that summer, neither of them able to satisfy my craving. I was beginning to realize that this drug wasn't working. I started to experience depressive episodes more frequently than I had in a while. I knew that I needed that high again, but I needed something more than these men were able to provide. That's when I met Paul. I knew of him because he was an old childhood friend of my brother. Paul had recently returned from the military and was a bit lost. He was looking for a job and my brother was able to give him one. By this time, I was seventeen and Paul was twenty-four. He was a handsome man; Hispanic, five foot nine, dark skin, black hair, brown eyes, built well, and strong. His smile was warm and genuine. He was kind hearted and loved to laugh. I was attracted to him from the start. He drove a light duty tow truck and I was cleaning the offices for my mother when I wasn't working for the PI. I enjoyed hanging out with him; going on tows with him. We laughed a lot. At first, he just thought his friend's little sister wanted someone to hang out with. And at first, that's all it really was. My sister and her friends could be boring at times and I didn't have anyone else to hang out with. So, in the beginning, it was innocent enough. But the more time we spent together, the more my addiction rose to the surface. The first time we expressed our interest in one another was when we were traveling back from the San Augustine Mountains on a tow. We drove down the popular highway, listening to music and talking about life. I blurted out that I liked him as more than a friend. He smiled his gentle smile and told me that he too felt the same. We held hands the rest of the drive. There were a lot of things to be afraid of. His age, the fact that he was my brothers' friend, and the fact that he worked for my family's business. We knew we would have to keep it a secret. I suppose that contributed to some of the excitement; the fact that it was a forbidden relationship. But we dove in anyway.

I remember everything about him and the time we spent together. He added the element that was missing from my drug; love. We had fun when we were together, and we rarely fought. The excitement of our forbidden love added to the satisfaction in the bedroom. It was a dangerous combination for someone always looking to get high. Paul never made me feel dirty or cheap. He made me feel like I was the only person who mattered. We had big dreams of a perfect life together; marriage, kids, the whole package. He was offering something the others had not; the fairytale. He was the prefect drug; the one that lasted all day and long into the night. I quickly became a part of his family as I had done before with Jacob's family. Paul's parents were wonderful people and welcomed me in with open arms. They were kind and treated me like one of their own. We even took family pictures together and there I was, hanging on their wall. I had never been on someone's wall before. It was everything I ever wanted. They made me feel, for only the second time in my life, like I belonged.

When my parents found out about our relationship, they were furious. My mother called me while I was in school to fire me. The rule was, no fraternization amongst employees. Because his position was less easily replaceable, they chose to fire me instead of him. I wasn't all that upset about it. I loved Paul and if I couldn't work as the cleaning lady at the offices, well, I just didn't care that much about it. By this time, I didn't want anything to do with the family business anyway, so being fired was just reassurance that I didn't belong there.

When we first started dating, he was living at home with his parents. We didn't have much in the way of privacy. So about four months in, he found an apartment on the west side of town. It was a one bedroom on the third floor. But I didn't mind the stairs. We played house well and could be alone in our fantasy world without the reality of his parents constantly pressuring us to grow up and face responsibility. I would go straight to his house almost every day after school. I had no desire to be anywhere else. On the weekends I would spend the night. I don't know if my mother even realized that I didn't come home. Paul became my whole life; my only comfort; my only solace; my favorite drug.

At Christmas I forced him to ask me to marry him. I know it was forced because he didn't even get the words out before I said yes. I assumed that he wanted what I wanted because we had talked about it. Looking back, I can see the uncertainty on his face as he held that ring, desperately searching for the words to go with it. He was my fairytale ending and everything I ever wanted. I believe he loved me; but I don't know if he was ready to marry me. He knew how screwed up I was, how could he not? His age and maturity gave him an advantage that I didn't have. I can only imagine how much pressure that must have been for a man like Paul.

During the year we spent together, he only hurt me once; over my High School Prom. I wanted to go so bad; perhaps just to check it off my list or perhaps to show off this man that I loved so much. But he was twenty-four years old and extremely uncomfortable at the idea of going to a high school dance. It was clear that he felt much guilt over hurting me and I could see that he wanted so badly to take me. But we did something else instead. He handled it well and with love, proving to me that he was of pure heart and kind in nature.

He was there when I graduated high school and he was genuinely proud of me. His family was proud of me too. By this time, my dad made no attempts to hide how much he hated Paul. The fact that he was Hispanic was enough for my father to want to make Paul disappear. But I didn't care. I never saw color or race when I was with him. My dad hadn't been in my life for years, so I didn't believe he had any right to say or feel anything about it. I only saw the love and the life that Paul had to offer me. During my graduation party, my dad spent the entire time pouting in the garage with the family attorney. I was embarrassed and humiliated; not just for me but for Paul too. And why had my dad shown up anyway? As far as I knew, I still wasn't his daughter.

I moved in with Paul days after graduating high school. My mother didn't even notice I had left. We found a cute one-bedroom condo close to my brother's house. By this time though, Paul was starting to figure out that I had no idea how to be an adult and he had no idea how to teach me to be one. We quickly began to struggle, and I refused to get a job. Emily Rose had come back in to the picture and was starting to pressure me about being too young to be in such a serious relationship. She wanted me to go out and have fun with her. Paul had already had his fun and was ready to settle down. I thought I was ready to settle down too, but the words of Emily Rose echoed in my head as they always did, and I started to question every move I made.

I was over dramatic about little things he would say to me. Looking back, I realize that he simply needed me as much as I needed him. He was afraid of losing me and what we had. Maybe I was his drug. I became selfish and started to feel like he was smothering me. Ironic considering that I had smothered him for so many months before. I started spending more time with Emily Rose and ignored his pleas for us to just be us again. I caused him to have unnecessary expenses and put us in a very bad financial state. But I didn't care. Suddenly the drug wasn't enough, and I was out of control. And I certainly wasn't about to allow him to take control. Unfortunately, I was knee deep in a downward spiral and neither one of us realized it. Suddenly, my perfect drug was no longer enough. Within a month of living together, I cheated on him with Markus Stone; my go-to, the one I could not seem to get out of my head. The guilt I felt was overwhelming. I didn't tell Paul right away. I told myself that it was a onetime thing and that I could live with the guilt and work harder to be a better fiancé. I never meant to hurt him. But I did. I definitely did.

No matter how hard I tried, Paul couldn't get me high anymore. I felt guilt and shame every single day. Self-loathing took over and I was desperately looking for a way out. I wanted him to be the bad guy so that I wouldn't have to face the truth about myself. I projected all my feelings of worthlessness and guilt on to him. Yet, he stood tall and took it all on. He was true to me, true to himself, and as faithful as faithful gets. He had made a commitment and he wasn't about to break it.

It was a harmless conversation. I was his fiancé, he was in love with me, and all he wanted was to be happy again. He had called me and told me that he wanted to take a drive that evening after work. He wanted to go back to the highway, where, for the first time, we had expressed our feelings to one another. He assured me that everything was going to be okay. I reverted to my manipulative ways and took the opportunity to play on my sister and my mother's sensitivity. They didn't like Paul much and I had already convinced them that he was controlling. I played scared at the notion of going anywhere with him alone; pretending to be afraid that he was going to hurt me. It was simple to sway them and without question, my sister helped me move all my stuff out while Paul was at work that day. We quickly packed everything up in the back of our pickups and were out of there within an hour.

I broke his heart. I knew I broke his heart before he did. I hated myself before we ever left the condo. I knew that what I was doing was wrong. But I did it anyway. He called me later that night, begging me to come home. He was lost. He knew that I had a spare key to my parents' house in the door of my truck. He showed up, probably around midnight, and let himself in the back door. We sat on the couch; we both cried, and he begged me to come back. I told him that I would. But I rushed him out of the house when I heard my mother wake up. She came out right after he left. I had to maintain the lie and told her that he broke in to my truck and broke in to the house. I was shaken up, but it wasn't because he had been there; not in the way she thought. I was shaken up because I knew I had made a mistake and that my life would never be the same without him. I knew I was a bad person; I just didn't know how I had become such a bad person.

My mom called my dad and told him what had just happened. Unbeknownst to me at the time, my dad went to the condo and confronted Paul. He punched him in the face and then had him arrested for trespassing. I found all of this out the next day when I finally spoke to Paul again. There was a distinct flatness in his voice as he told me what my father had done. My dangerous addiction had broken him. I knew it; I heard it. That night, my dad stayed at the house in case Paul tried to come back. I knew he wouldn't. I knew, after that phone call, that he would never be a part of my life again. As I got ready to go to bed, my dad looked me straight in the eyes and said, "Maybe next time you'll be more careful of who you sleep with." My heart broke in half. I was a whore and my dad knew it. I went to my bedroom and cried. I cried for Paul, I cried for Jacob, and I cried for myself. I didn't want to be bouncing around from man to man. I wanted everything Paul had promised me. I wanted to be married. I wanted kids. I wanted the fairy tale. I wanted Paul. But boy did I screw it up once I had him.

I never heard from Paul again. He eventually got married and had a child of his own. I tried to contact him a few times to apologize and seek his forgiveness. But it was too late. If he ever forgave me, I'll never know. I had nothing to forgive him for. He did everything right. It took me over twenty years to forgive myself for the pain I caused him. But I believe he is happy now. That was all I wanted for him. He deserved happiness. And though I regret all the horrible things I did to him, I do not regret being with him. He was an integral part of my life. He and his family cared for me and helped see me through a pivotal time. I am eternally grateful to them and I am eternally grateful for Paul, the one who got away.

CHAPTER 11
DANGEROUS GAMES

I had a nightmare before my session with Christina one week. I was anxious to talk to her about it and get her thoughts. As I explained that the nightmare was more than a dream, it was in fact, a reality that haunted me now and again, she listened intently and thought hard before she spoke. "Do you think you were drugged?" She asked. I didn't know. Maybe. What I knew was that it haunted me and not knowing the exact details made it that much more terrifying. I had never told anyone else but Christina about it. At some point in my life, I concluded that it was my fault for living in danger to satisfy my addiction and that I had no right to talk or think about it. But the nightmares didn't go away until I told her.

****

After Paul and I broke up, I began spending all of my time with Emily Rose. She hadn't changed much over the years. She still felt compelled to insult my clothing, my hair, my weight, and well, everything about me. But she had been around since that day on the playground and I couldn't bring myself to stop being friends with her. She was wild and was always full of bad ideas. But my desire to belong somewhere often clouded my judgment of doing the right thing when I was with her. She was all I had after Paul and doing dangerous things with her was better than doing nothing.

She wasted no time pointing out the five pounds I gained when I was with him. She informed me that I had already been overweight for some time and needed to get a handle on it before it got too late. We went to a store in a questionable part of town and she bought me a bottle of pink hearts. Over the counter speed. How easily she convinced me that I needed to be thinner. Truth be told, I was only one hundred thirty-five pounds and five foot eight. I was in fact healthy. But not in the eyes of Emily Rose. The first pill went down easy and within an hour I had an unusual amount of energy. It was like being drunk without the alcohol but add in the jitters. I secretly contemplated the idea that this could replace my addiction and I was immediately hooked. Incidentally, I lost ten pounds rather quickly.

By this time, I was eighteen, living at my parents' house again, and no longer had a curfew, though, I'm quite certain my curfew went out the window when I started spending nights with Paul. Emily Rose and I would go out almost every night. She would always drink and get stoned, so I took on the role of caretaker. I made sure she didn't go home with random men and I made sure she didn't drive. I was there for her, despite her constant insults and despite the incident that occurred right before Paul and I broke up.

For my eighteenth Birthday, Emily Rose and I had gone on a road trip to a popular lake out of State. When we arrived at the camp site on the lake, it started to become clear that this was not going to be the weekend I thought it was going to be. She was meeting up with some friends, people that

I believed were bad news. It seemed that I was simply her only means of transportation and that was why I was invited. I tried to blow it off and just have fun. What I got instead was a glimpse into the true character of Emily Rose. Upon our arrival, we quickly discovered that the four-wheel drive in my truck was not working correctly. We parked it and hopped in the back of her friends pick up. We set off to go cruising down the beach. Within minutes, I was thrown from the back of the truck and hit my head on a rock as I landed. By the time I got my bearings, Emily Rose and her friends were gone. They made no attempt to check and make sure I was okay. That is when all the anger from all the years of her abuse came out. I thought, in that moment, that I was done with Emily Rose. I walked the mile back to my truck and I left. I have no idea how long it took for her to realize that I had left her in another State, but I didn't care.

I wish I could tell you that was the last time I spoke with her. But clearly, it was not. We reconnected after Paul and I broke up and so enters over the counter speed and nightly parties. Between her and the pink hearts, I was successfully keeping my cravings under control. My dad had decided that he wanted to move back home and offered me a deal. He would give me a job at the family business so I could afford to get an apartment of my own. Essentially, he would move back in if I would move out. I jumped at the opportunity for freedom and found a tiny one bedroom in the same complex as my sister. I was going out every night with Emily Rose and working every day in the Accounting Office at the tow company. Though I was on my own, it didn't feel any different than the previous four years of living with my mother. I was simply in a smaller space.

I continued to take the pink hearts and once I had lost enough weight to be considered acceptable for Emily Rose, she announced that she was going to reward me by taking me out to the local Country Bar on family night. She took me shopping for a new outfit that she herself picked out. She insisted on doing my hair and my makeup. When I looked in the mirror, I wasn't sure who the girl was that was staring back at me. But Emily Rose approved and concluded that her transformation of me would get me a man that night.

My stomach was doing back flips when we arrived at the bar. I hadn't been with anyone since Paul and I broke up. I hadn't even thought about being with anyone. I partially listened as Emily Rose barked instructions at me. "Don't laugh hard, you look stupid when you do that." And as we walked under the sign that said, *"Country Dance Bar"*, "Don't dance, you are a terrible dancer. If someone asks you to dance, tell them you can't." Basically, what she wanted was for me not to be myself. Once we entered and after we waited in line for over an hour to get a soda, we began to make the rounds. I would have been perfectly content to find a table and sit, but she insisted that we walk around the bar, in circles, until we found what she was looking for. By the end of our second round, I saw him. His style was different, but the cowboy hat and boots didn't change the man underneath. It was Jacob Dean; flirting with a table of beautiful women. My heart stopped. My stomach turned. My head began to spin. I was certain that I was going to faint. I ran toward the bathroom with Emily Rose at my heels, clearly confused and unaware of what was happening. Once I threw up and was able to explain to her why I had just experienced the first anxiety attack of my life, she rolled her eyes at me. I cleaned up my face and a nice woman let me use some of her mouth wash. By this time, Emily Rose had concluded that this was the perfect opportunity for me to show Jacob what he had lost. With that, we went back to making our rounds only this time, the goal was to make sure that he saw me looking good that night.

After an hour of walking in circles and watching Jacob

pick up on damn near every girl in the bar, I convinced Emily Rose that it was time to leave. We went back to her house and settled in on the living room couch. I allowed myself to be vulnerable with her and I told her about my feelings for Jacob. I explained that I had never quite gotten over him and I missed him terribly. Seeing him brought back all the pain that I had been avoiding with my addiction. It was then that she began to tell me a story about her friend named Jody whom she used to hang out with in High School. She told me that Jody starting dating Jacob right after he graduated. She told me how they had made fun of me because I was so pathetic for trying to get him back. She told me intimate details about Jacob's room and the gift I had given him for graduation. The details of her story placed this Jody girl in Jacob's life before he and I had broken up. So, what Emily Rose didn't know, or care to know, was that she was telling me that my Prince Charming may very well have cheated on me. My wounds were reopened, and she merely laughed about it, as if it meant nothing. I was crushed and fighting back tears. I wanted to storm out of the house, but that wasn't me. Instead, I sat and listened quietly as she recited the jokes they made about me. Even after that, I continued to hang out with Emily Rose.

I met Keith while she and I were out cruising. It was common place for us to drive to a small town to the north of us and cruise the strip in Emily Rose's mustang. It just happened that Keith was there with some friends that night and she knew him from high school. Somehow, I was able to get his phone number and we started talking. I believed he was out of my league and Emily Rose made every attempt to confirm that belief. Since that night at the Country Bar, my cravings had come back and were becoming overpowering. I had all but stopped taking the pink hearts because they were starting to have side effects. I knew that I didn't want to continue old behaviors, but I thought maybe I could tweak them and still survive. If I could find a nice boyfriend, like Paul, who would give me the satisfaction my body had come to rely on but treat me well too, it would all be okay.

Keith and I went on a couple of normal, dinner type dates. He was so handsome; tall and thin with a face like a Greek God. Blond hair, blue eyes. He was exquisite. Unfortunately, he knew it. He spent more time in front of the mirror than I did and I'm pretty sure he spent more money on hair products too. His taste in music was dark and one might argue that he was a troubled teen. But he was cute, and he hadn't pressured me to have sex with him. He didn't care much for Emily Rose and asked me if I had any other friends. He told me that his best friend James had just broken up with a girl. He thought it would be nice if I could set him up with one of my friends to cheer him up. I remembered a girl I went to high school with named Angie. Having met James a few times, I knew she would be perfect for him. She seemed genuinely excited to hear from me and eager to meet James. We went on a couple of double dates and things were going well. Or so I thought.

One night we all met up at James' house. They had managed to get us wine coolers, so our plan was to hang out, drink, and watch movies. The night is very foggy for me. The details I remember are terrifying. We walked through the house toward the back. Angie and I met James' mom. She was a short round foreign lady. I think she was Polish. The house was a ranch style home with a finished basement. That was where we would spend our evening. It was set up with a living room and what appeared to be some extra bedrooms. The colors were reds, oranges, and blues. When we reached the bottom of the stairs, I could see the wine coolers on the coffee table. There was some conversation and laughing as we drank. The next thing I remember is waking up to light shining in my eyes. I was laying naked on a bed in one of the bedrooms. James' mom was at the door scolding James and pointing to me. Both James and Keith were in the room. My crotch hurt; I reached down and touched my throbbing vagina only to pull my hand back and see blood. I remember both Keith and James leaning over my body. I remember Keith finger banging me while James watched. I was sore and there was no doubt that I had had sex. I just wasn't sure with whom I had had it. The next thing I remember was waking up on the couch at Keith's house. I had no idea how I got there, and it was very early in the morning. I was confused and left without asking any questions.

The next day, I wanted answers. I was sore but could only see quick images that ran through my head. James and Keith had both done things to me, but I didn't know exactly what or for how long. I had only drunk a half of a wine cooler, so I knew I wasn't drunk. Keith wouldn't answer my calls and after days of trying, it was clear that he had no intention of providing me with answers. Angie finally called me a few days later. She told me a story about Keith and James that made my blood run cold. She informed me that, for years, the two had been playing a game where they would see how many girls they could get in bed and how long it would take them to do so. They each had a belt on their headboard and whomever got the girl in bed first, got to put a notch in the belt. It was a race between them. Keith was winning. James told Angie this because he didn't want to play the game anymore. She said that he admitted his love for her and told her that he didn't want anyone else but her. Her tone was cold and her attitude, uncaring. She, in essence, broke up with me for Keith. I never saw or spoke with any of them again.

I will never know what really happened that night. I only have my broken, foggy memories to rely on. I know, in my gut, that whatever did happen, wasn't good and it wasn't with my consent. After that, my heart turned to stone. My soul became vacant. I stopped talking to Emily Rose completely and made no attempts to make new friends. I was full of anger and contempt. I was angry that I allowed Emily Rose to treat me poorly for so many years. I was angry for not knowing what happened that night at James' house. I was angry for hurting Paul. I was angry at Jacob Dean and the mere idea that he may have cheated on me. I was angry at my parents for being absent. I was angry at my brothers' friend. I was angry at Mr. Arke. More than anything, I was angry at this desire within me that was constantly whispering in my ear; telling me that it would all go away if I would just go find Markus. But I didn't want to. I fought the urges and allowed myself to withdraw from the all the people in my life. I wanted to find a new way to numb the pain. Solitude was all I could manage.

CHAPTER 12
NOT MYSELF ANYMORE

If I learned anything from Christina, it was that there is an underlying cause of all the mistakes I made throughout my life. She challenged me to think about what led me to my decisions and helped me understand how that related to my trauma. Though I am a firm believer that there is no justification for bad behavior, I do believe that if you know the root cause of a problem, you will be better prepared to discontinue the bad behaviors. Christina had become my life coach and taught me how to be better prepared for almost everything.

****

As the winter of my eighteenth year began, the cravings, once again, started to consume me. I needed to find something else that would satisfy my addiction but wasn't sure what that was or how to find it. It would have been easy to seek out Markus again, but I couldn't bring myself to do it. I had a moment of clarity and recognized that perhaps part of my addiction was due to my desire to be loved by my dad. So, I threw myself in to my work and discovered that this brought about a sort of acceptance from him. The idea that I might get my dad back sparked my interest and quickly became my sole focus. I spent my time getting to know my co-workers and doing whatever it took to prove to my dad that I was good. That's when I met Brad. He was older than me by six years and after Keith, I went back to my previous notion that boys my age were just not right for me. Brad was a driver for the family business who had just moved here from the west coast. I wasn't attracted to him at all. He was shorter than me with brown hair, thick round glasses, and a round face. He wasn't my usual type. He seemed to lack basic common sense and drove me nuts with his spelling. But still, there was something about him that I liked. He was a dreamer. An adventurer. I believe it was his drive to reach his goals and his belief that he could conquer the world that attracted me to him. He was a drifter and I, so badly, wanted to be a drifter too. At first, he expressed interest in my sister. It made perfect sense. They shared much more commonalities than he and I did. From their spiritual beliefs to their hobbies; they would have been what his mother considered to be the ideal couple. But my sister, being one who refused to rock the boat, wouldn't break the business rule - no fraternization amongst employees. And I, being the rebel I was, didn't have any problem breaking the rules.

When we first started talking about hanging out, it was under the premise that we would just be friends. In our minds, this wouldn't completely break the rule. But as these things go, the friendship clause was quickly broken. The first night we hung out we took a drive and talked about what we wanted to do with our lives. We were both full of hope and big dreams. The moment we crossed the line from friends to lovers we were pulled over on a quiet two-lane highway a short way outside of town. His door got locked and I leaned over to unlock it for him. There was a look in his eyes when he got back in the car that told me he wanted more. Something inside of me sparked and I realized that it had been a long time since I had gotten high. I knew him well enough from our time together at work to know that he was safe. That was a quality I needed after Keith.

After a week or so of endless flirting at work, long gazes, and subtle hints, we had a second date. I had given in to my craving and was anxious to be numb. I found myself in bed with him that night and it wasn't great. My mind didn't clear, and reality didn't slip away. He was a very selfish lover; offering quick and clumsy foreplay with no interest in making sure I was satisfied. It was unfamiliar territory and I wasn't sure how to proceed. I thought about it long and hard while he slept next to me that night. He couldn't offer me the high I needed and that was hard to move past. But I didn't want to be a whore anymore. I wanted to be different. I was intrigued by his drive and his passion to reach his goals. He was safe and I believed he could offer me stability. By the time I fell asleep, I decided that I would give it a try and see where it went.

Between work and Brad, it seemed that I had figured out the formula to keep my cravings at bay. Brad and my relationship was a lot of fun at first. I enjoyed listening to him tell me about his dreams and found myself wanting to fit in to them. I quickly became a pro at faking orgasms because I wanted to make him happy. I didn't dare tell him that I found no satisfaction in our physical interactions for fear that he would leave. He was showing me new things and trying to fit me in to his way of life. I was the puzzle piece that got put away in the wrong box. But it was fun to pretend to be someone else after so many years of just being me.

After we had been dating for a few months, he told me he loved me. I froze. I told him I didn't love him. Not the way he wanted me to. While I enjoyed spending time with him and dreaming with him, I didn't have the feelings I knew I should have had for him. I convinced him that we could remain friends, with benefits. I could immediately see that I hurt him. Yet, he stuck around. He seemed to believe that he could change me and that I was afraid to admit that I loved him back. My cravings began to surface again, and I needed to find an escape from reality. No matter how hard or how much I worked, those old, familiar feelings began to take over. I knew there was only one place I could go that would provide me what I so desperately needed. Markus Stone. One hour with him and all the pain disappeared for days. I didn't dare tell Brad what I had done. I believed that what he didn't know wouldn't hurt him. But the guilt and shame I felt lingered over my head like a brick.

Brad and I continued in our "friends with benefits" relationship while I worked my way in to a better position with the family business. Our lives were consumed with work, bad sex, and ambitious dreams. But the whole, "I love you" thing lingered over our heads and placed great strain on the relationship. He told me he had applied to go overseas for six months on a job and I pretended not to care. It really did bother me, but I didn't feel like I had any right to protest. The truth is, I did love him, but I wasn't attracted to him and in my mind, that meant I couldn't love him. It didn't take long after that for our relationship to waiver and we eventually broke up.

I continued to throw myself into work; moved out of the apartment I was in and moved in with my sister. Brad was no longer working for the family business and I was sad that he was gone. I missed the companionship that we shared. I started hanging out with one of my co-workers who was much older than I. She was a nice gal, fun to be around and pretty down to earth. She was married and had two small kids but was young at heart and seemed to get me. I didn't have any friends my age, well, I didn't have any friends. Susan took me under her wing, recognizing that I was lost and needed someone to help me through. She went with me to get my first tattoo and invited me over for family dinners. It was refreshing to have someone new to hang out with, someone who was light years away in maturity from Emily Rose.

Not long after we started hanging out, Susan recognized that I was lonely and set me up with her husband's nephew, Frank. Her intentions were pure and the cravings inside me were taking over. Susan invited him and I over for dinner at their house. It was awkward at first. He was much older than I, probably around twenty-eight and we didn't have anything in common. After what seemed like an eternity of small talk, Susan and her husband went to bed. Frank and I stayed down in the family room and talked a bit; trying to get to know each other. He told me the story of why he had difficulty meeting women. If my body was trying to give me any signs that red flags were everywhere, my mind was ignoring it. Frank explained that he had been in prison for rape of an underage girl. He said it was all a bunch of bull and a huge misunderstanding. Given my history with over aged men, it didn't occur to me to consider that his side of the story might not have been true. Within a couple of hours, I found myself letting him touch me and undress me. The high was back; something I hadn't felt since my last encounter with Markus. I quickly lost touch with reality and succumbed to the drug. We made out for what seemed like hours before we completely undressed, and he moved on top of me. For some reason, I hesitated and started to move my hands toward his chest to push him away. He took my arms and pushed them back on the couch, holding me down; he was strong. He looked me in the eyes and said, "They told me you are a good girl. You are a good girl, aren't you?" I froze. I nodded and the story he told me just hours before began to run through my head like a broken record. I shut my eyes tight and focused on my breathing while he moved inside of me. When I opened my eyes, I didn't see Frank; I saw Mr. Arke. I was paralyzed with fear and quietly waited for him to fall asleep so I could escape.

I didn't see him again after that. I told Susan that he just wasn't my type and I withdrew from her. I had nightmares for weeks and found myself stuck in childhood memories. I sat with my pain alone and let it eat away at me. I searched inside myself for an answer. I wondered why I kept putting myself in dangerous situations. I knew my need for the drug was unhealthy, but I couldn't bring myself to stop. I was completely worthless and helpless against my addiction. I thought back to all the men I had been with and once again found myself thinking about Markus Stone. I believed that I could be completely satisfied with him. One man, one love, for life. I wanted to ask him to be with me. Really be with me. But when I got to his house, it was immediately clear that he wasn't interested in conversation. He led me straight from the door to his bedroom. The moment he touched me, all my pain disappeared. I was overcome with relief and anxious to tell him that he was who I wanted to be with. But when we were done, he didn't give me an opportunity to speak. He chatted about nothing as he walked me to the door as if he was avoiding any type of real conversation. For the first time, the high I got from Markus Stone wore off before I made it to my car. I was humiliated and realized that I was nothing more than a cheap whore in the eyes of Markus Stone. It was then that I realized that I could never see him again.

Reality hit me when I woke up the next morning and I knew that I needed to reevaluate what I was doing. I continued to throw myself in to work. I made proving myself to my father my sole purpose. I worked sixteen sometimes twenty hours a day. Part of my motivation was to show my dedication; the other part was to keep my mind occupied. I was lonely but afraid to go out and meet new people. The cravings became more of an irritant than a desire and I chastised myself constantly for having them. I made the demand on myself to become a better person and thought hard about what that looked like. In the end, I decided that Brad was the answer. During our time together, he made it clear that he had a strong desire to change me. I decided that if I couldn't change myself, I would turn to someone who could. So, I sought him out and begged for his forgiveness.

By that time, Brad was seeing another woman. He seemed to care for her a great deal, but said he cared for me more. He agreed to break it off with her and take me back, but I had to agree to give him one hundred percent. It was an easy promise to make. For once in my life, I was the one someone was choosing to love. I had never felt that before. But it was clear that he had strong feelings for her. That was visible in his eyes and his demeanor the night he went to meet with her to breakup. It was bittersweet. On the one hand, I felt like I had won the love lottery; finally, someone chose me. On the other hand, jealousy began to build inside of me when I thought about the look on his face as he left to go meet her. I became controlling and unbearable at times, always wondering if he loved her more and wanted her back. I didn't believe myself to be good enough for him, or anyone for that matter. I made every change he wanted in an effort to secure his love. My promiscuity was replaced with self-loathing, fear, and anger.

We moved forward in our relationship with one thing hanging over our heads; he was going overseas for six months but now, he was going with the woman he had broken up with for me. I think he thought that was the toughest obstacle we would have to face during his time away. What he didn't know was that while yes, them being there together worried me, my tendency to act out sexually worried me more. I was becoming aware of my addiction and was determined to overcome it.

As Brad's trip grew near, I moved out of my sister's and got an apartment of my own again. He spent most nights at my place and may as well have been living with me. It was during that time that I learned how often he drank and frequented strip clubs. I hadn't paid attention to any of that before. And it bothered me; a lot. We argued about it often. I confided in a co-worker, looking for confirmation that his behaviors were normal. She told me that as long as he was coming home to me, I should be happy. "He gets to see strange women naked and you get laid. It's a win-win" she said. As much as it hurt, I pushed on and remembered her words every time I began to feel insecure about it. When his final week at home arrived, I asked him if we could spend his last night together. But his friends wanted to take him out to the strip club for one last boys' night. We fought over that for days and inevitably, he chose the strip club; nothing I said was going to stop him. His decision cut deep, and I was left believing that I was unworthy of his love. When he got back to the apartment that night he was drunk and wanted sex. Regardless of what my coworker had said, I felt dirty knowing that he wanted sex with me only because he was turned on by strippers. I received the message that I was second best and would never be good enough for Brad. And yet, I chose to stay, clinging to the hope that he could take away my addiction and change me in to a different person.

I struggled with being faithful every single day he was gone. I occupied myself with work during the day and sending racy emails to Brad at night. I worried about the woman he was there with and questioned him often. He told me that his sister had sent him a large amount of porn to keep him faithful, so I had nothing to worry about. This made me remember the magazines I looked at when I was younger, and I was immediately overcome with shame. That only made me worry more; strippers and porn were not things I had been exposed to in my relationships with men. I thought those things were for single men and wasn't necessary once they found someone they loved. This only confirmed for me that I wasn't good enough. His desire to look outside of our relationship for excitement and my dissatisfaction in the bedroom made me question if I could overcome my cravings while he was gone. But somehow, I made it through those six months faithfully, without falter. I had overcome an obstacle I wasn't sure I could clear. But I did and the conclusion I came to was that he must be the one. The real one. When he returned, nothing was different. The sex still didn't take away my pain, and he was still going to the strip clubs despite my objections. But I was convinced that he was the only way to find purity. We decided we would move our relationship to the next level and officially moved in together. I wanted to be the woman he wanted; someone that wasn't me.

CHAPTER 13
THE WEDDING

"Do you understand what a narcissist is?" Christina looked thoughtfully toward me. She went on to explain that I had been exposed to a great deal of narcissism throughout my life. Though I had knowledge of the term, I would never have applied it to any of the people in my life before my journey through recovery.

****

Brad and I settled in to a routine quickly. He started working for the government and I was still working for the family business. He knew most of the details regarding my family dynamics and he supported my decision to continue working there, despite my motive. Though most days, I was miserable. My dad was still my dad. He yelled a lot and threw things. In fact, one night, when I was training a new dispatcher, my dad was angry about something and started throwing three ring binders at me. I remained calm and simply moved my body to dodge being hit but the new dispatcher fled the property in tears. I simply laughed and went about my work. I had become numb to my dad's outbursts and couldn't see how inappropriate they were. My vision was clouded with dreams of gaining his acceptance. Brad wanted me to quit but said he would support me in whatever decision I made. He knew that in my heart, I didn't want to be there. I had told him of the promise I made to myself when I was seventeen that I would never work for the family business again. He believed that it would be up to him to help me fulfill that promise. But neither he, nor I, understood that he was not capable of helping me. His form of help was to simply change *me*. Change my body, change my habits, change my way of thinking; change all of things that made me, *me*. It didn't occur to me that conforming to his ideal was wrong. That realization took years. At that time, I wanted to be anyone but me and I didn't want to lose the only person who seemed to love me. My insecurities were running my life.

Everyone worked for the family business: my mom, dad, sister, brother, sister-in-law, aunt, uncle, and cousins. You name it, they had a job there. But there was a certain sense of comfort that came with that. I guess some of that had to do with growing up in it; the whole comfort zone theory. For me, it became an easy replacement for my addiction. The more Dad yelled, the more I tried to appease him. The better I did at my job, the more accepting of me he seemed to become. I wanted him to love me and I thought that I had finally found the true formula. It was far from perfect, and there were many obstacles. My brother and his wife Val being the largest ones. I found myself fighting with them on a constant basis and just wanted to get away from them. But the idea of finally having my dad's approval was always there, pulling me back.

When Val came in to the picture when I was thirteen years old, she seemed nice. Always smiling and showing care for others. I thought she was one of the coolest people I knew. It's easy to see the surface of another person and be deceived in to thinking that's who they really are. But when you really get to know people, especially family, you break through the surface and the inside starts to become visible. I'm not sure when I became her target. My brother and I didn't get along well so perhaps that was the underlying issue. No matter what I did, she would complain about me. I could make the smallest most meaningless mistake and she would make a mountain out of it. She was just like Grandma.

The power struggle between my brother, his wife, and I became way more than I could handle at twenty-one years old. The effects of our arguments were taking their toll on my parents as well. On top of the internal issues with us kids, they were having issues of their own with my choice to move in with Brad. Though they did like him, they didn't like me being with him. We had violated policy (even though he was gone by this time), and I was young. They seemed to think that I needed to hold out for the perfect man though I wasn't entirely sure what their idea of perfection was. The daily struggles became unbearable and my still rebellious mind wanted to escape. Eventually, the disagreements with my brother and Val became too much for me. So, I quit. In my family's business, you don't just quit your job. If you quit, you are quitting the family too. I didn't realize that until after I had done it.

Suddenly, I was disconnected from my family and had no friends. My sister and I talked on occasion, but she was building her own life too. All I had was Brad. He was encouraging and supportive at first, as I tried to figure out what to do with my life. He introduced me to all his friends and tried to get me to form friendships with their girlfriends or wives. I didn't have anything in common with them and felt out of place. He was making minimum wage and doing everything in his power to support the both of us. I remember how proud of myself I was because I could buy a weeks' worth of groceries for twenty dollars. It was a tough road, but one we needed to travel for growths sake. In addition to working full time, Brad did volunteer work for a local organization. He would go to work at his day job early in the morning and then go straight to volunteer when he was done. On nights and on weekends, he carried a pager with him that would alert him if there was an emergency at work; he was always on call. There were a lot of emergencies, so he was gone most of the time. Our relationship started to become mundane and predictable. Brad's goals and dreams were the priority. Sex was almost non-existent and didn't offer the clarity I craved so badly. In my mind, I thought that meant he was falling out of love with me. So, I tried harder. I became obsessed about my body when he told me that he preferred a woman who was toned. I wasn't fat by any means, but I wasn't toned. I thought that if I could get my body firm, he would want me more. I was doing it for the wrong reasons, so it was easy to give it up when his desire didn't improve with my level of fitness. More and more he was gone; losing track of time at work and hanging out with all his single buddies. I started to become frustrated with him and myself. It seemed as though I was just not doing it right because no matter what I tried, I could not get his attention. I began to withdraw and would spend endless hours in our bedroom playing video games and watching MTV. I knew I needed to get a job and move on with my life, but I had become invisible to the only person I had contact with. The time spent at home, alone, only allowed for old feelings to surface. I began to fall in to a deep depression believing that I was unloved and completely alone.

Whether Brad recognized my state of mind or not I don't know. But at one of my lowest points, he came home and announced that it was time for me to meet his parents. He had requested the time off work, and we were going to drive across country to go meet them. I was excited for a road trip and was anxious to have time with him. The idea of meeting his parents gave me joy. I never once considered that they might not like me. After all, Jacob and Paul's parents loved me. In my mind, I had nothing to worry about.

On the drive out there, Brad and I talked about his dreams and goals for our future. It was nice to hear him dream again; it had been so long since we talked like that. But when we arrived at his parent's house, it was apparent that his mother and sister did not like me at all. I wasn't sure what I had done to make them hate me since I had never met them before. But their distaste of me became painfully clear the moment I walked through their door. The trip rapidly turned stressful and I found myself overwhelmed with sadness. Brad thought it would cheer me up if he introduced me to some of his ex-girlfriends. When I questioned him on how exactly that was supposed to cheer me up, he informed me that if I was going to be with him, I would need to accept the fact that he would be remaining friends with his ex-girlfriends no matter what. That was that and I was not given room to voice my opinion about it. I reluctantly withdrew my argument and met his exes. It was more than awkward and close to humiliating. And just when I thought that was the worst thing that could happen on our trip, we went to dinner with his entire family.

After everyone ordered, his mother began talking about the girl Brad dated while we were broken up. She, very sincerely, told me that Brad loved that girl with all his heart and was devastated when they broke up. Despite the obvious look of shock on my face, she continued to explain to me how that girl was the love of Brad's life. My eyes swelled with tears and I politely excused myself to the bathroom. While I stood in front of the mirror, taking deep breaths and wiping my face, Brad's sister came in to inform me that I needed to suck it up and be nice. She advised me that they did not like me and that if it weren't for me, her brother would be back home with them. Before we left the bathroom to return to the table, it was clear that she and her mother were going to take steps to remove me from Brad's life. I was blown away. It was like nothing I had ever experienced before.

I told Brad about the interaction I had with his sister and he agreed that we would cut our trip short and return home the following day.

Once we were settled back in our condo, life continued, status quo. Only, I was lonelier than ever before. The trip left me heartbroken and reopened wounds from my past. Words echoed in my head like a broken record and I couldn't escape them. I found myself at my wits end and finally threatened to leave if life did not change. I didn't know where I would go, but I knew I couldn't continue living the way we were. We had been together for years and there seemed to be no clear future for us. I wanted something concrete; something that assured me, one hundred percent, that he loved me and wasn't going to leave me. The result of that threat was a marriage proposal.

It was not well planned nor romantic, but I found ways to justify his seemingly heartless proposal. It was my twenty second birthday and we had little money. He told me I could have anything for dinner that I wanted. Thinking economically, I chose Dairy Queen because a chili cheese dog and a blizzard sounded good. I'm not exactly a high maintenance woman. I had no idea he was going to propose so when he got on one knee over my chili cheese dog, I was caught off guard; but thrilled that he wanted to make the commitment. We began wedding preparations right away. I finally had something to keep me occupied. It wasn't until a few months after the proposal that I became bitter about it. He had a friend who was going to propose to his girlfriend but needed help because he was planning something grand. Brad spent many hours helping his friend prepare for and execute that marriage proposal. I found myself, once again, feeling unworthy and concluded that Brad must not believe I deserved such extravagance. I didn't want to seem ungrateful, but I couldn't let it go. It followed us through the duration of our marriage.

The year before our wedding went by rather quickly. Once we announced our engagement to my parents, they slowly started talking to me again. I found a job working in police dispatch and was making good money. We bought our first town home and my parents helped us with some of the repairs. Things were looking up and life was taking on a feel of "normal". But as the wedding drew near, I found myself falling in to old habits.

After working at the PD for a couple of months, I developed a crush on one of the officers. Though I held my ground and did not act on my cravings, I found myself flirting endlessly with him, night after night. I told myself that it was just pre-wedding jitters and that it wasn't harmful. But I thought about that officer a lot and I wondered if I was making a mistake marrying Brad. The routine at home hadn't changed; he was always at work or volunteering and I was working graveyard shifts. We rarely saw each other. I convinced myself that that was what adult relationships were like and I needed to get over it. I feared that if I said anything to him about it, he might not want to marry me anymore. So, I found excitement in flirting with hot cops and became an expert at masturbation.

The week of our wedding, many of Brad's family and friends began to arrive. One of his friends was an ex-girlfriend. She had moved on and was married herself, so her husband was with her. But for whatever reason, that woman hated me in a way I never understood considering I had only met her, briefly, once before. She arrived the Thursday before our wedding and when she walked in to my house she was rude, disrespectful, and refused to talk to me. I had never encountered anything like it before. Regardless of whether my parents were right or wrong in the way they raised us, we were always taught to be respectful of other people in their homes. Up until that moment, I thought everyone had been taught that. Brad spend the entire evening on the patio with her and her husband while I sat on the couch trying desperately to understand what I had done wrong. When I confronted Brad about it before bed, he defended her actions and refused to see how it made me feel. I cried myself to sleep in defeat, unsure of how to handle the situation with no back up. Little did I know, that would be the first of many nights I would cry myself to sleep.

The following evening was our rehearsal dinner. We held the event at the club house in our complex. It wasn't much, but it was cute, and it was cheap. Brad's parents had food catered in and all our family and friends had arrived. As we were making the final preparations, I overheard Brad's mom and his ex-girlfriend having a heated conversation about how much they didn't like me and how Brad was making a huge mistake. I panicked and hid around the corner; my heart pounding loudly in my chest. One of Brad's other friends' girlfriends caught me in tears and demanded that I tell her what happened. I didn't know her well, but she was a kind woman and she comforted me as I told her the story of what I had overheard. She helped calm me down and convinced me to go mingle with the other guests. She stayed by my side until she knew I was okay and comfortable enough to mingle on my own. Throughout the evening, Brad could only be found with his ex-girlfriend and their mutual friends. Eventually they all ended up by the pool and I was left alone inside to entertain both families. I was emotionally drained and finally used the excuse that I needed to get some sleep because I didn't want to have bags under my eyes on my wedding day. Luckily, that stuff was important enough to my mom that she agreed whole heartedly and told me to go home and rest. Brad didn't even notice that I was gone. He stumbled in to bed, drunk, sometime in the middle of the night making no attempt to be quiet. I cried myself back to sleep, wishing that the whole wedding would just be over already.

Brad's oldest sister arrived the next day; our wedding day. She did nothing but insult my sisters' abilities to perform her duties as the Maid of Honor and tried to take over. Brad's ex-girlfriend pretended to be supportive, not realizing that I had heard every mean word the night before. I was stressed out and because of that, so was my Maid of Honor. At one point, everyone was in the dressing room with me, my sister, his sisters, his ex-girlfriend, the photographer and maybe the mothers. Overwhelm took over and I started to cry. The photographer made everyone leave except my sister. I stared in the mirror and verbalized how ugly I was. She wanted to take pictures of me in my lingerie, but I wouldn't have it. I stood there, on what was supposed to be one of the happiest days of my life, staring into a full-length mirror, wishing I was someone else. Prettier, thinner, more fun, more outgoing, more lovable, worthy, and more like his ex-girlfriend. In that moment, all the hate that I had developed for myself over the years was staring back at me. I wanted to run as far and as fast as I could. Instead, I cleaned myself up, met my dad at the back, walked up that aisle, and said "I Do."

The ceremony was beautiful and if anyone was complaining, I didn't hear it. I was nervous and a voice inside my head was screaming for me to run. But I fumbled through and it was over before I knew it. As Brad and I drove to the reception venue, he talked about how excited he was for our party. I pretended that I was excited too, though, all I really wanted to do was go home. The events leading up to our special day had taken their toll and I was afraid of what might happen next. Rightfully so.

As the reception got going, everyone seemed to be getting along okay and I thought that maybe I could relax a little. We still had some pictures to take with the wedding party but for the most part, we were at a point where we could enjoy ourselves. Right before dinner was about to be served, there appeared to be some commotion going on with my brother and sister-in-law. I tried to ignore it but when the photographer came over and asked if we could finish up the wedding party pictures, I had to go find them. After a few minutes of searching, I was told that they had left because she was upset. The story goes that my new brother-in-law had a bit too much to drink and was hitting on my brothers' lovely wife. She got upset about it and even more upset when my brother laughed it off as no big deal. She would not let it go and they left; without saying goodbye. Anger and sadness overwhelmed me. I sat back down at the head table and cried. Not so much because they left, more so because I was afraid that the reception was going to turn as bad as the previous few days had been. And I wasn't wrong.

After dinner, the DJ had Brad and I come up to the front of the room so we could get ready for the garter toss. He wanted my dad to come up too, but they couldn't find him. The crowd went silent as the DJ was calling for my him and my new mother in law yelled, "He's probably on his phone somewhere, he's always on his damn phone." Her voice was dripping with disdain. My face turned a dark shade of crimson and once again, tears swelled up in my eyes. Turned out, Dad was just at the bar. The DJ gave Brad the choice to take the garter off with his hands or his teeth; while my dad stood there, watching. I begged Brad to take it off with his hands, but he chose teeth. As he lifted my dress, I was overcome with shame and humiliation. I know it was meant in fun but given my past and the self-hatred I had been feeling, I didn't find it entertaining whatsoever. I was hurt that Brad hadn't considered how it would make me feel to do something so personal in front of a large group of people with my dad standing less than two feet away.

The best moment of the whole wedding was when I tossed the bouquet. My cousin literally pushed people down to the ground as she went in for the catch. That was entertainment but more than likely because the person who was pummeled was my new sister-in-law. But the evening, unfortunately, got worse. At the very end of the special dances, we decided to do a money dance. This was where all the men and women lined up to dance with the bride and groom. They gave you money and then danced with you. Not one of Brad's friends, of which there were many, got in line to dance with me. In fact, only a few men in the crowd lined up to dance with me that night and most of them were friends of my family. They recognized that my line was short and most danced with me more than once to comfort me. Once again, my eyes swelled with tears and I was overcome with humiliation. When I tried to pull Brad to the side and talk with him about it, he blew me off like it was no big deal and only wanted to complain about the talk he and my dad had. It was a typical dad talk, don't hurt my daughter or I'll hurt you, etc. Nothing out of the ordinary from what I knew about dad talks. But that was Brad's only focus; that and drinking with his buddies.

By the end of the evening I was emotionally exhausted and just wanted to go to our hotel room. I didn't want to mingle anymore, and I certainly didn't want to have sex. I just wanted to get out of that dress and get the hell out of that reception hall. Brad didn't want to leave but one man, who was a friend to the both of us, helped convince Brad that it was time to leave. He accompanied us to our room and did his best to cheer me up. He had witnessed the unfortunate events of the day and knew that I was sad. It was the only nice gesture I witnessed that day and one I will never forget.

Our wedding night was nothing special. We didn't consummate our marriage and I cried myself to sleep once again. It would become just a typical night being married to Brad.

PART 3

FAMILY OWNED AND OPERATED

"In troubled families, abuse and neglect are permitted; it's the talking about them that is forbidden." ~Marcia Sirota

CHAPTER 14
FOR BETTER OR FOR WORSE

"Have you ever heard the term "gaslighting"? Christina cocked her head and waited patiently for my answer. I was clueless and must have had a puzzled look on my face. As she explained the term, my mind began to race, and memories began to flood in.

****

Things settled down once all of Brad's family and friends left town. We drove to Las Vegas for a short honeymoon; yes, we did that all wrong. It was nice to get away from all the negativity. We were okay together when it was just us and our dreams. Most of our conversations centered around what our life together would look like if he could reach all his goals. It was a quiet trip and by the time we were ready to leave, I was no longer dwelling on the train wreck that was my wedding. When we got home, my brother asked me if I would come back to work for the family business. I was tired of working the graveyard shift and worried that I would succumb to old habits and do more than flirt with the hot officers. After a couple of days, I said yes. It felt good to be needed, even if it was coming from my brother.

During our first year of marriage, Brad accepted a position with a local police department, and I got pregnant. I had been working twelve hour shifts most days and was doing everything I could to maintain the new-found acceptance I was gaining from my dad. When I announced my pregnancy, my parent's reaction was not what I thought it would be. My mom rolled her eyes and said "great" or something equally unenthusiastic. My dad said "oh goodie" in a disapproving tone. I didn't understand why they weren't happy for me. I had done it almost the right way; met the boy, bought the house, got married, having a baby. I couldn't wait to be a Mom. I just knew I would be good at it. But my parents didn't believe the same. My mom told me that she thought I would be a bad Mom because of how selfish I had always been. Her words cut me to the bone, and I wondered if I would ever be good enough for her.

But as my due date approached, my parents began to warm up to the idea of having another grandchild. I had gained a great deal of weight, but I didn't care. I was happy as could be that I would have someone to care for in a way I myself had never been cared for. I planned to stay home with the baby for at least the first year. I was thrilled that I was finally living the fantasy. It wasn't perfect, but it was far better than the life I was living before I met Brad.

When my son was born, life changed in ways that no one ever prepared me for. He was a good baby but as babies go, he didn't sleep much, and I was exhausted in my new role as a Mom. While Brad had a lot of time off, he did work long shifts that generally fell on the nights that I questioned if I knew what the hell I was doing. But about eight weeks after the baby was born, things were starting to settle down. I figured out a schedule that worked for everyone and we were adjusting well. I felt truly happy for the first time in years and thought nothing could bring me down. Our town home had three bedrooms upstairs; the baby's room, our room, and an office. One day, I went in to the office to look for something and noticed a piece of paper on the desk with pictures printed on it. As I looked closer, I realized they were pictures of naked women in very sexual poses. My mind was pulled back to visions of penthouse and playboy. I was overcome with emotion and my stomach flipped. Angry, I turned on the computer and pulled up the Internet history. Staring back at me were hundreds of pornography websites. I knew those sites existed; I simply had no experience in viewing them. Despite my promiscuous history, I hadn't viewed such pictures since I snuck upstairs when I was a little girl. I was hurt and a bit disturbed by the images before me on the computer. Though, considering Brad's flippant attitude about strip joints and pornography in the beginning, I shouldn't have been surprised.

I confronted him with the pictures later that evening when the baby was asleep. His response echoed in my head for years. He looked me dead in the eyes and said that he needed "something good to look at." My body turned cold and my heart stopped beating. I didn't know what to say. I didn't understand how my husband, who was supposed to love me unconditionally, could say something so mean, so horrible. It never occurred to me that he was dissatisfied with my appearance. I was still hosting a considerable amount of baby weight and was self-conscious enough for the both of us. But I had no idea that he didn't find me attractive anymore. So much so that he felt the need to turn elsewhere to get his kicks. Something inside of me changed that night; my method of thinking shifted. My already warped sense of self and what love was, turned darker than I knew was possible. I gave up any sense of self-worth I had left. That night started me on the path of compromising everything I believed in my core.

Over the next couple of years, we bought a house with

a yard and I was able to continue to stay home with the baby. I started feeling the cravings again but fought them off by trying to find new ways to please my husband. I didn't want to go back to being that girl. I concluded that if Brad wasn't interested in me anymore, I could incorporate pornography into our sex life so that he would stick around and stay satisfied; even if I was not. By the time our second child came around, I had become a master at knowing exactly what turned my husband on and how to keep him from looking at porn without me. I thought that if we were doing it together, it would be less harmful.

I learned from the "experts" in those movies how to properly perform all things sexual. We began using toys and exploring unique forms of pleasure. I hated myself. My days were filled working part time at the family business and completing my motherly duties. My nights were spent trying to be a porn star. I was out of control and life was becoming miserable. I confided in my brother of all people about some of the issues Brad and I were having. His response only added to the suitcase of lies I carried with me in my head. He told me that if your spouse wants you to look like a super model, then you need to do whatever it takes to look like a super model. I then turned to a male co-worker to ask if porn was okay and he told me that men were visual creatures and that there was nothing wrong with it. My suitcase was getting full.

I could sense that the enhancements I was making in the bedroom weren't enough for Brad. He still found me unattractive. He made that clear with little comments here and there if we were leaving the house. He wanted me to wear black because it slimmed me; he wanted me to wear my hair down and make sure I had makeup on. Perhaps these were meaningless suggestions that he thought were helpful. Maybe they were in fact, innocent in nature. But they stuck with me and echoed in my head every time I thought of my husband looking at porn because I wasn't good to look at. All the negative messages I had received in my lifetime played over in my head like a broken record. I was afraid to lose him. I knew that if I did, I would become that girl again; moving from random guy to random guy. And now I had kids; this complicated everything.

I continued to compromise myself and my core values to maintain a happy home for the kids. I took Brad to a gentleman's club for his birthday one year. Our daughter was one or two at the time. I think I thought if I was there with him, I could control the situation. But it didn't change the horrible feelings I had inside as I watched him watching those women with lust in his eyes. I figured out quick not to watch him while he was watching them. So, I started watching them and that's when I turned back down that dangerous road that I was all too familiar with. I was confused by the feelings of excitement I had as I watched the women strip. But as I turned back to Brad for answers, he was looking at me in a way he had never looked at me before. My excitement had only made him more excited. The sex that night was the best it had ever been. Yet, I still went to sleep feeling guilt and shame. The pressure of providing the kids what they needed and providing Brad what he needed was beginning to wear on me.

Due to the added financial responsibility of another child, we agreed that I needed to go back to work full time. My parents had an opening and I was all too eager to take it. The time at work gave me a break from the reality of my responsibilities as a wife and mother. I was exhausted by bedtime and found that simply taping a Penthouse Centerfold to the wall and letting Brad do me from behind was the easiest way to get him off quick so I could go to sleep. I felt dirty and cheap every time we had sex but was too tired to care. I had lost control of my body and fleeting thoughts started to enter my dreams. That's when I started to think about other men again. At first it was just a fantasy of finding a man who found me attractive the way I was and wanted me and only me in the bedroom. But because I was me, allowing those thoughts allowed the addiction to resurface. Before I knew what was happening, I was relapsing.

Dominic Rivers was similar to the men I had pursued in the past. He was short, had long hair, and was kind of an asshole if I'm being honest. But he drove a motorcycle and his eyes; I cannot find the words to describe to you how his eyes brought me to my knees. We would have entire conversations just with eye contact. The cravings were back, and I didn't want to stop them. It had become a more dangerous game this time around. I was married and he worked for my family. This drug was better, different than before. I began to work longer hours so that he and I could flirt. I dreaded going home to my husband who seemingly could not get an erection unless porn was involved. I began behaving like a teenager again. Though I was careful to ensure that my kids were getting my attention; I began to withdraw from Brad. I found myself not giving a damn if he watched porn without me and in fact, I got to the point where I could not have sex with him unless there was some sort of extras involved. I simply held no attraction to him anymore, only contempt.

But when I was hanging out with Dominic, I didn't need those things and neither did he. He was interested in me, well, in sex, but I took that to mean, just me. We engaged in verbal foreplay for over a year. He played games with me and I played right back. We would sext during working hours and toted the line when he was in the office. If Brad was at work or away from the house, we would talk on the phone. We had fights like regular couples, though we weren't one. When we made up, we would pick right back up where we left off. There was an unspoken understanding that he was not willing to sleep with a married woman, but he was willing to keep her occupied until such time that he changed his mind. It kept my cravings at bay, for a little while.

By the time my daughter was two and my son was five, Brad and I were in financial distress. Even though I was working a lot of hours and bringing in decent money, the years of me not working had finally caught up to us. We were house poor, having entered in to a bad loan. We eventually lost our home and moved in to one of my parents' rental properties. Brad wasn't happy about it. Since I went back to work for the family business, my parents had become a big part of our lives again. I let them in wholeheartedly and left room for them to guide us through our troubles. Brad didn't like that and expressed that they were too intrusive in our personal business. Despite his opinions about it, he knew it was the only way for us to survive. I fell back in to the old habit of working hard to prove to my dad that I was worthy of his love. I didn't dare express to him my dissatisfaction in my marriage. I wanted out, but I didn't know how. Not without disappointing my dad and messing up my kids.

I was out of control and trapped. The desire inside of me was the worst it had ever been. I felt powerless over it. I began falling in to depressive episodes more often than ever before. I had gone back to therapy a couple of times, only to be told that I was Bipolar and needed medication. My gut told me differently; I was still not being honest, and the diagnosis went ignored. Brad couldn't handle my depression and turned to my mother for help. Of course, that didn't get him anywhere. She simply told him that I was his problem now and that she did not have any desire to help him. He yelled at me because of her response. Like it was somehow my fault that my mother was who she was. He got angry with me for being depressed and said I just needed to get better. I slowly started to realize that Brad could not change me the way I had hoped he would. The only way I knew how to be better was to allow the cravings to be satisfied. I thought I was beginning another downward spiral, not realizing that I was still in the middle of one.

I did anything and everything I could to occupy my time. I worked long hours, flirted with Dominic, and got overly involved in my sons schooling. I thought I could occupy the depression away and avoid completely giving in to my cravings. I made a new friend for the first time since high school. Her name was Nora Boyd; I met her at my son's school. She was older than I was, but we seemed to have a connection. Brad didn't like her, though I had no idea why. It was nice to have an outsider in my life for a change and she was kind to me, so I didn't care much what Brad thought. But no matter what I did to try and occupy my mind, nothing took away the overwhelming feelings of needing the drug. I started thinking about Markus again and tried to find him, though, I was unsuccessful. I was completely lost and needed a change and the universe always had a way of presenting me with what I needed.

CHAPTER 15
ASSISTANT OPERATIONS MANAGER

Christina understood my desire to be accepted by my dad despite the toxicity of it. "Do you understand why this is so important to you?" I understood why and I understood the damage it did to me. Even at the time I think I understood that it was unhealthy. Despite that knowledge, I made it my focus anyway.

****

My brother and I had never really gotten along though, I wasn't exactly sure why. There were times when we worked well together, however, it never lasted longer than a few days. I believed that his wife, Val, was the source of our turmoil and she somehow always confirmed that belief. If my brother and I began to get close or agree on business matters, she would concoct some crazy story about things I had been doing wrong and my brother would immediately be angry with me again. No matter how many hours I put in or how well I did my job, she seemed determined to bring me down. I often wondered if she was whispering in my dad's ear the way Grandma had when I was a child; telling him stories and lies to keep him from loving me. It seemed as though I would always be bad in my family's eyes. Yet, I was set on changing their view of me and I was determined to find acceptance where I had always been rejected.

It was 2005 when my dad bought a second company. It was located much farther away than where we lived and was about a forty five-minute drive in nice weather. I was the last to be told about the purchase, but the first to step up and offer to help. I wanted to get away from my brother and Val. I wanted to breathe without them in my space. So, I begged my dad to let me help him with the new shop. For whatever reason, it didn't take long to wear him down and by my twenty ninth birthday, he agreed to transfer me.

I started out as his assistant. We shared an office and I did anything and everything he asked me to do. I helped in dispatch when I was needed and made friends quickly with all the employee's there. The atmosphere at that shop was much different than what I had been used to. People enjoyed their jobs and they operated as one big family. Something I had never known before. They worked together in harmony and helped each other during weak moments. I could see why my dad had kept the employees that he did. They were loyal to the company and wanted only to see it succeed through the change. I fell in love with the environment and wanted nothing more than to prove to my dad that I could run this company better than anyone. It was the change I had been looking for. Finally, I was one on one with my dad and I could prove to him that I was worthy and maybe, just maybe, that would be what it would take to finally make him love me.

I worked tirelessly to show Dad that I was capable and worthy. The drive was long and when I would get home, I would offer what little energy I had left to the kids. This meant that I had nothing left to give Brad. Our relationship continued to be vacant of any real substance. Though Dominic and I still spoke frequently, we didn't see each other anymore. I was completely occupied with the business and the kids. And when that wasn't enough to fight off the cravings, I would add more to my plate. I continued to volunteer at the elementary school and tried to find time to spend with Nora. I made sure that Sundays were spent at my parents' house to foster a relationship between them and the kids. It was also a way for me to show my dad that I was willing to do more than just work for him the way my brother and Val did. I wanted the whole package and didn't understand why they did not. It was obvious that our Sunday routine bothered Brad, but my contempt for him had become indestructible and my rebellion toward him was much like that of a teenager. I wanted to hurt him the same way he had hurt me.

Despite my attempts to keep busy, the cravings lingered. I was feeling acceptance from my dad, but I wasn't feeling loved at home. I had thought that winning my dad's love would create some formula that would make it so that I didn't need my husband's love. It didn't. Even though I had lost some weight, I was nowhere near the body Brad wanted. When I looked in the mirror, I hated the person staring back at me. I only saw a woman who believed she was ugly, fat, and unworthy of good things. I was a bad person and I didn't deserve happiness. Sex continued to require props and if I complained about it, Brad would only offer ideas on how I could change the situation so that I was more satisfied. Just as it was when I was a child, the problems were my fault because I had somehow failed to be good enough. No matter what I did, I couldn't measure up.

I was blind to the fact that I needed to seek help for my depression; blind to the fact that my desire to act out was deeply rooted in pain from a childhood full of monsters and rejection. Though I continued to busy myself with the kids and various work projects, the desire to be loved differently wouldn't leave me. Once again, I became consumed with dreams of being rescued by Prince Charming. Only this time, I was playing with frogs and none of them would transform upon true love's kiss. Dominic and I began talking again when the kids were in bed and Brad was at work. He maintained his stance that he would not sleep with a married woman, however, talking still wasn't an issue. I desired him but more so, desired an end to the cravings. I thought that if I could have just one fling, the need to fulfill my addiction could be kept at bay for a longer period. After all, I had gone years without succumbing to my weakness. I reconnected with a man I had been friends with in Junior High. After a few phone conversations, we met, and I found myself in bed with him. The encounter was unsatisfying and left me feeling only shame. The craving was still there and even worse than it had been before. I became consumed with finding the perfect drug and reached out to a former co-worker whom I knew would be willing to mess around. But he was not the answer either. I only felt shame when we were done.

Desperate and completely unable to see the damage I was doing, I convinced Dominic to come over one night when he was drunk. It was around two am, after the bars had closed. He was easily seduced and as he entered me, that overwhelming feeling of clarity engulfed me. Finally, I had the drug I was looking for. But the high was short lived. When I woke the next morning, the shame had created yet another bleeding wound deep within my heart. I promptly fell into a major depressive episode. I couldn't get out of bed and called in sick to work for days. Something inside of me told me that I could redeem myself for what I had done, if I focused on nothing else but my husband, my kids, and my job. I made a promise to myself that I would never speak a word of my infidelity to anyone and I would sever all ties with Dominic. I was desperate to find good within myself and began spending all my free time doting on Brad. I stopped trying to talk to him about our problems and did whatever he wanted in the bedroom. His overall satisfaction in our marriage became yet another project to keep me occupied.

When I looked in the mirror, I saw a fat, ugly, whore. I knew that I would never be worthy of the type of love that I believed was out there. I realized that I was bad, and I wanted to change and be good. But I didn't know what that looked like. I decided that simply being faithful and busy would be the key to finding the answer. After a few months, the cravings had subsided, and I was able to stay focused on my new mission. That's when Brad and I unexpectedly became pregnant again. I was elated but my parents were not. Dad was giving me more responsibilities at work and a baby meant that I wouldn't be able to fulfill the duties he had in mind for me. Determined to prove him wrong, I continued working long hours and assured him that a baby would not interfere with my career goals. I endured great stress during the seven and a half months I was pregnant and lost weight. I continued smoking throughout the pregnancy, something I had not done previously. I assured myself and those around me that everything was going to be fine and life was going to change for the better.

Life did change for the better. Though my little guy was born six weeks premature, he was healthy. Colicky, but healthy. I only took a two-week maternity leave before I returned to working long hours. We had good, reliable child care and Brad seemed to enjoy having the extra time alone with the kids. Somehow, this dedication to work gave my dad the proof that he needed to start a new conversation. I was going to be the new assistant operations manager. It was what I had been working so hard to attain; acceptance. The man I had lost so many years before finally saw me. The new title meant additional hours; I would be on-call at night and would be expected to make big decisions. I was ecstatic that Dad believed in me to make those decisions on my own. He had never believed in me before. My worthiness was finally defined.

That's when a competitiveness I had never experienced before began to surface. My new mission: prove that I could run a company better than my brother. He and I hadn't been working closely together as the two shops functioned separately. This was my chance to show Dad that I was better; that I could build his empire to a new level in a way my brother could not. The resources I had at my disposal were great and my employees were loyal. I knew that if I presented them with an idea of growth, they would work with me toward the goal. I made sure to treat them all with respect and maintained an open-door policy. I listened to their ideas and suggestions and found creative ways to present them to my dad for approval.

Though I continued to throw myself in to my work and my kids, something was still missing. I was living my dream; husband, kids, house, and my dad's acceptance. But inside, I was hollow with nothing more than a beating piece of stone so cold that even the hottest summer day could not warm it. I continued to battle my appetite for the drug by preoccupying myself with more tasks. When that wasn't enough, I would try desperately to engage Brad in sexting for the sake of maintaining fidelity. Though, nothing worked, and I found myself, once again, looking outside of my marriage for the piece of me that was missing.

Neil was one of my drivers and that meant danger. He was different than Dominic though. He seemed to understand what I needed. It hadn't occurred to me previously, but he pointed out that what I desired was to be seen. We talked for hours on the phone at night when the kids were asleep, and

Brad was at work. We discussed our dreams and aspirations of a different life. I confided in him the secrets I held so deep inside. He didn't judge me; he didn't scorn me. It felt good to be vulnerable with him. He made it very clear in the beginning that we were just friends and despite our attraction to one another, he refused to be the person who broke up a marriage. Somehow, that was enough this time. His friendship kept my hunger at bay. But the closer we got, the harder it became to ignore the growing attraction. We talked about what that looked like and Neil was clear that he would only pursue a relationship with me if I left my husband. We both knew I wasn't ready for that and reluctantly, we agreed that we had to end it. My heart of stone suffered another crack; just enough to bring me back to the darkness. The only way to repair the damage was to dive in to yet another project. That's when my dad volunteered to help coordinate the state industry trade show. The Tow Show.

CHAPTER 16
THE INDUSTRY

"I imagine it made you feel good to belong." Christina's smile was always so genuine. I felt like I belonged when I was with her. But yes, being part of something so big satisfied my desire to belong. Being around the best of the best in the towing industry gave me the impression that I had arrived. I was someone that my dad and my brother could be proud of. Someone worthy of their love.

****

When I was a little girl, I remember going to the Tow Show. It was always so much fun; they had boardwalk games that we would play for prizes. I'm sure they had adult things going on as well, but all I remember were the activities they had for us kids. It was a fond memory. My dad always seemed to have his hand in the coordination of the shows. I can remember being at a woman's house, though who she was, I cannot remember. There were boxes all over the floor of her living room and she and my dad would spend hours working on the Tow Show. The rewards, for me, were great. It was one of the few times in my young life that I remember feeling happy and feeling like part of the family. So, when my dad volunteered to bring back the show, I was all too happy to help. I wanted to recreate the memories I had, and I needed another distraction from the pain that had become a part of my soul.

I paired up with one of my dad's best friends, a man that had been part of our lives since I was little, Walter. He owned a small company in a city about twenty miles from us and was just as heavily involved in the association as my dad was. We shared the same vision for the show and quickly became partners in crime. He was easy to talk to and listened with great interest when I told him of the struggles I had with my dad. He was encouraging and supportive. Always willing to teach me how to run the trucks, what to look for when buying a truck, etc. All the things my dad didn't think I needed to know how to do. Walter became the father I never had. Together, our excitement about the show escalated and we knew that if we were partners, the show would be great.

Brad seemed jealous of Walter and every time I came home from a meeting it was as if I was entering the Spanish Inquisition. I told myself that I deserved to be treated that way and would answer the same questions over and over with humility. Brad didn't know the extent of my betrayal, but I did. I knew every dirty secret and no amount of preoccupation could lighten my soul.

Being a part of the Tow Show meant being a part of something important; the association. My dad had always been an active member of the State Towing Association. It made him seem big; infamous. I wanted to be a part of it and show everyone how infamous I could be as well. Bringing a show back to our State was a big deal and if I could make it successful, everyone would know me, and I would become important too. I threw myself into the task at hand. Walter and I had grandiose dreams of going regional and the baby steps we needed to take were often grueling. We just wanted it to be big then, in those first moments.

Our first show went off without a hitch. In fact, it was the first and last time I heard my dad tell me he was proud of me. I was on top of the world. We had pulled off a very successful show and I was certain that nothing could take away my dad's acceptance of me. It was, in my mind, the ultimate victory.

Things at home were proving to be tough; Brad and I were simply surviving. I had come clean about my affair with Dominic. Brad insisted that we move and get away from the house where I had been unfaithful. Which we did. I let him take the lead and pick the house he wanted. It was his dream home and I wasn't interested in taking away any of his dreams. I had done enough damage already.

My dad was very angry when we announced that we were going to move. He wanted us to stay in the rental and save up more money. Brad wanted my dad to stop getting in the middle of our business. I just wanted everyone to be happy and approve of me. I had become a people pleaser and did everything in my power to keep the waters calm on both fronts. I continued to work long hours to prove my worthiness to my dad. While the kids were awake, I would do my best to be the greatest Mom I could be. When the lights went out and the kids were in bed, I did my best to make sure that Brad was satisfied. Even if that meant being tied up to the railing downstairs, whipped, choked, bruised, or providing on demand blow jobs. He took pictures of me during our encounters. One time, he posted a picture of me blowing him on a swinger's website. He said he was going to have the control over my infidelity and that I had no right to argue it. I no longer had jurisdiction over my own body. I was expected to simply accept his terms and my deep-seated guilt over-road my ability to defend myself.

During this time, I started to develop a deeper friendship with Nora. She and I seemed to understand one another, and I felt like I could tell her anything. She offered to help me with the show and quickly fell in with our industry family. Walter and I continued to work tirelessly to ensure the show's success. I was becoming more popular within the industry and everyone seemed to think highly of me because of my talent as the show coordinator. Somehow, being part of the upper echelon within the industry helped me push through the emptiness of my marriage. But then, Walter got sick. It was determined that he was going to die and there was nothing I or anyone could do about it. He had become my second father and the very idea of him not being there left me lost and scared. But it was inevitable, he was admitted in to the hospital and was quickly going downhill. Brad accused me of sleeping around every time I went to visit Walter. I'm not sure if he thought I was sleeping with Walter or if he thought I was lying about how sick Walter was to cover up for sleeping with someone else. Regardless, I did my best to brush it off. After all, I deserved it considering what I had done.

After what seemed like forever, though it was only a couple of months, Walter passed. Whatever light was left within me went black that day. Brad got angry at me for going to the hospital to see Walter on his death bed. He said I was spending too much time there and didn't believe that's what I was really doing. That was it. My stone-cold heart broke in half. Any possible connection I had left with Brad was severed.

The last conversation Walter and I had involved him asking me to promise him that I would find happiness. I made the promise and I knew that I wouldn't be able to keep it as long as I stayed with Brad. That night, my body was numb, and my mind was blank. Something inside of me changed. I could feel the coldness of my heart; the brick it had become. I was oddly aware of my vacant soul and began to wonder if I was irreparably damaged. But making that promise to Walter ignited something inside of me. Something I hadn't felt in I don't know how long; hope.

Walter's funeral wasn't the first I had attended in a tow truck, but it was one of only a few that held profound meaning to me. The procession was long, the line of tow trucks, beacons turning, stretched about two miles. I drove in silence, allowing my mind to give in to overwhelming sadness. Being a part of something so acute was incredibly surreal. The clarity I experienced when I succumbed to the drug hit me out of nowhere. I didn't know I could experience that level of lucidity without being high. I knew what I needed to do but I wasn't sure how. I was only certain that I was ready.

CHAPTER 17
THE ULTIMATE DRUG

*Though Christina revealed many things to me, she was not the
one who verbalized that I had an addiction. Perhaps I knew it
all along and was simply denying it. It took writing this book
and embarking on a journey of healing for me to realize that I
had a problem. And when I told Christina what I had
discovered about myself, she wasn't surprised.*

****

After Walter's death, I continued to coordinate the show in
his honor. I worked harder and was determined to make the
show what Walter wanted it to be. My feelings toward Brad
were non-existent. I was empty when he was around. I closed
myself off to him and focused on nothing more than the tasks
of being a wife, Mom, and career woman. I was a robot, going
through the motions to satisfy everyone else; including a dead
man. That's when I let my addiction take over.

I met Shane in the height of Tow Show season. I was
stressed out and had a head cold that left my face red and puffy.

He needed a job and I needed a driver, so my appearance was not at the forefront of my mind. I remember telling him that I didn't want to shake his hand because I didn't want to get him sick. He was incredibly handsome, six-foot, brown hair, brown eyes. A little bulky around the waist but his broad shoulders and strong, tattooed arms made up for that. And he drove a motorcycle. I hired him on the spot; not because he was a hot bad boy but because he was qualified, and we needed qualified. I didn't truly recognize my attraction to him until a few days later, when my head was clear of mucus. All the girls in the office were ecstatic that I finally hired a good-looking man. "Eye candy" they called him. By this time, I was longing for what Neil and I had but with more. It didn't matter how hard I tried to ignore the urges of my addiction. They were there, inside of me, and I had no idea how to make them go away.

I realized how strong my attraction to Shane was when I was checking students in for classes at the show. He was helping the instructor out and as he stood back in the shadows, I could feel him watching me. His eyes followed me closely from behind his sun glasses causing a fire to ignite inside of me. Thoughts of him consumed me and I struggled to focus on my duties as the Show Coordinator. I was enrolled to take the very class he was assisting with. It was awkward and I was aware of every move both he and I made that week. Suddenly I was a teenager again; trying desperately to impress him while maintaining an air of sophistication. I was cautious to keep my motives from being revealed to those around me. It was a dangerous game and the high I got from playing was like nothing I had ever experienced before. It was a new level to my addiction; one I didn't know existed. The stakes were higher than they had ever been. By the end of the week, I was thoroughly captivated by Shane Andrews.

The classes came to an end and the show itself began. Shane didn't stick around for the weekend events which left me to tend to my duties with less distraction. The show site had a campground, so Brad brought the camper out for Nora and me. This made it so that we wouldn't need to travel back and forth every day. The show was early to rise and late to bed, so it was in fact a great plan. We always served alcohol during our evening events so having the camper within walking distance meant Brad could drink as much as he wanted for the first time at the show. Having just lost Walter and feeling a great deal of animosity toward my husband, I wasn't in a good head space about our marriage. Add to that the pure exhaustion of running the show; and sex with Brad was the farthest thing from my mind. By the time we got back to the camper that Friday night, he was drunk, and I was tired. Nora was sleeping in the back, a mere ten feet away, so I honestly didn't think Brad would want sex. But I was wrong. I tried to stop him and reason with him. I explained that I was uncomfortable with the idea of having sex while my best friend lay in bed so close to us. I begged him to let it go and even teared up. But he refused to listen and forced himself on me anyway. Humiliated, I simply gave in and for the first time, I was relieved by his inability to last longer than a minute. He promptly rolled over and fell asleep. I lay awake, my body trembling. I stared at the ceiling and allowed thoughts of Shane to warm me as I fell asleep.

Nora never said anything to me about that night, and I genuinely appreciated her silence. The next day I was angry with Brad for drinking too much and forcing me to do something that I was uncomfortable with. But Saturday was the busiest day of the show and I had no time to convey to him my disgust at his actions. Each time the anger surfaced, I simply reminded myself that the show was almost over, and things would be back to normal by Monday. That night I was again, exhausted and anxious for the weekend to end. As my dad and I stood to speak to the large crowd in the banquet hall, he called my husband up because they had a surprise for me. I did my best to hide the contempt brewing inside of me when my husband got down on one knee and proposed marriage to me. I turned my head away from the crowd as I whispered yes. The only person who recognized the look of pure mortification on my face was Walter's daughter, Shannon. I knew this was Brad's last-ditch effort to try and save our marriage. He explained to the crowd that he wanted to make up for the proposal he didn't give me the first time; the one that lacked the extravagance I had longed for. I was in shock; my mind went blank and I didn't have the courage to look him in the eyes and tell him the truth. I could only muster up the ability to do what was expected of me in that crowd. I accepted the ring, gave him a quick kiss on the lips, and hugged him in front of everyone I knew. Only Shannon seemed to understand that it was all an act.

The following day, I was too tired to bring up the humiliation Brad had subjected me to during the show. Perhaps I was also aware of the excitement he felt about the proposal and didn't want to crush him. It was clear that he was proud of himself and that he felt as if he had won. I pushed my anger down inside me and let him enjoy his high. The days that followed were less stressful which made it much easier to succumb to the familiar feelings of danger and excitement. I found myself creating reasons to see and talk to Shane. My desire for him seemed to be strengthened by Brad's gross display of affection at the banquet. I was acutely aware of every thought, feeling, and emotion that ran through my body when Shane was around. I tried to tell myself not to let it happen again, but my logical mind wouldn't listen. I allowed my emotions to take over and I surrendered to the cravings inside of me. I wasn't sure if he felt the same and needed to test the waters. One afternoon, while he was talking to the office clerk, I mentioned that I was feeling unusually fat and ugly. Shane spoke up and told me that I wasn't and that I shouldn't speak so harshly of myself. We gazed into each other's eyes for a moment and the door to danger blew wide open.

Our first interaction outside of work took place that afternoon via Facebook Messenger. I sent him a message thanking him for making me feel better. He sent me a message back telling me that what he said was simply the truth and it wasn't intended to make me feel better. We messaged each other back and forth several times that day and at some point, exchanged phone numbers. It exploded from there. While we were at work, we found reasons to cross each other's paths while exchanging knowing glances and flirtatious smiles. We would text each other frequently throughout the day and would talk on the phone if Brad was at work. Shane was recently divorced and seemed to understand where I was at in my marriage. I told him every dirty secret about myself without concern of judgment. He was kind and understanding even though his ex-wife had cheated on him. He didn't let my infidelity reopen his wounds. We were becoming close friends and by the end of those first two weeks, we found ourselves playing with fire. We hadn't so much as brushed arms - not even a hand shake - and we were feeling love for one another. The conversation was intimate, and tears filled my eyes as I began to speak. I started to tell him that I was confused by what I was feeling. When he asked what that was, I stopped myself from saying the words. But he said them for me. We both lacked the ability to understand how we could possibly love each other given our short time knowing one another. We agreed that we were brought to each other for a reason but also agreed that what I was doing was wrong. He knew that I didn't want to be this person anymore. That I didn't like the woman staring back at me in the mirror every morning. I didn't recognize her because she was not who I set out to be. Despite all of that, neither one of us were willing to give up the hurricane of emotions that was circling our heads. I no longer had a desire to control my cravings and he no longer wanted to help me control them.

The first time we touched was behind closed doors in my dad's office. I had pulled him in to talk about something I'm sure was made up. I locked the doors and I approached him. Our eyes met as he stood and leaned in to me. His fingers danced along my upper arms moving slowly toward my shoulders. An electric shock moved through my body, shattering the rock that encased my heart. His lips touched mine and my body went limp. Butterflies multiplied in my stomach and my skin tingled from head to toe. My mind cleared and every bit of pain disappeared. I knew, in that moment, with absolute certainty, that Shane Andrews was the ultimate drug. A drug I didn't know existed; a drug I never wanted to be without again.

After that, our conversations became consumed by lust. We tried to figure out the dynamics of meeting in person without entering in to my marital home. But our desire got the best of us and the first two times we were together ended up being exactly there. He took great care to ensure that I was properly satisfied each time. I hadn't been with anyone like him since Markus Stone. But the high I got from Shane Andrews didn't dissipate in between encounters. It was as if the first injection was all I would need for the rest of my life. Guilt and shame were replaced with clarity and vision. For the first time, I realized that I had a choice to be someone else. I could be the girl I set out to be and the only person who could change me was me. Shane and I had a connection that seemed spiritual in nature though I rebuked that idea given my knowledge of God's will. But still, there was something significantly different about this affair. Being with him made me want to be a better person. Being with him made me want to be pure again. Being with him made me want to change.

I confided in Nora and Shannon about my situation. Nora offered me comfort and understanding. Shannon offered me help and a plan to move forward. By this time, Shane and I had been having an affair for just over a month. I was trying to figure out the dynamics of Shannon's plan, but he was getting anxious and overcome by guilt for being the other man. He started to pull away which gave me the push I needed to act. There was only one right thing to do and that was to let Shane go and come clean to Brad. But something inside of me couldn't let that happen. Maybe it was the addiction or maybe it really was something spiritual. The only thing that felt right was Shane.

I was exhausted from the lies and trying to figure out how to do the right thing for me. Shannon helped me enact step one of the plans and one night I confronted Brad. He was standing in the kitchen and I was sitting at the table. I asked him if he was happy. He told me no and followed by saying that he knew he'd be happy someday though. I was sad for him, knowing that he was willing to accept a life of unhappiness. I was sad for me, knowing that I couldn't make him happy. In a voice even I didn't recognize, I told him that I wanted a divorce and that I had already secured an apartment. I would be moving in a week and there was nothing he could say or do that would change my mind. He was, by all rights, furious and hurt. I couldn't bring myself to tell him about Shane. Brad deserved to be free of the pain I caused him over the years without injuring him further. I needed to find the good person inside of me; the honest and pure woman that I knew was waiting to be introduced to the world. I couldn't be that person with Brad.

We argued for hours and I finally lied and told him that I was going to stay with Shannon for the night. Fear overwhelmed me as I drove away. I had no idea what life would look like moving forward but I knew that I had done the right thing. For the first time in years, my blood ran warm and my heart beat strong. Hope was building inside of me. I went straight to Shane, the man I believed to be my soul mate. When I arrived and told him what had just occurred, I could sense that something inside of him had changed. His body language whispered guilt and uncertainty. My gut told me that something was wrong, but I ignored it. I had just left my husband to be with him and there was no way I was willing to entertain the idea that maybe I had made a mistake.

CHAPTER 18
THE ART OF BETRAYAL

"It sounds like Shane is very supportive of you and that the two of you have a solid relationship." Christina was looking for confirmation of her assessment. Yes, Shane was a supportive man who would do anything for me. But there was a time when I didn't think he would stick around. A time when both of us were so broken we could only hurt one another.

****

Within days of my leaving Brad, word spread quickly throughout the industry. My parents were furious and showed little support at first. My brother expressed his disappointment by warning me that I was making a poor decision for my kids. Only my sister, Shannon, and Nora offered me the support I needed. Drivers started picking up on me left and right; as if it was somehow open season on dating me. Shane and I had done well to keep our relationship quiet and if anyone knew about us, they didn't let on. But something had changed in him. He was withdrawing and seemed as though he no longer wanted to be with me. He was becoming secretive and my gut told me that he was seeing someone else. But I ignored my gut; Shane was my ultimate drug and the future didn't look right without him. Somehow, I had concluded that ignoring what was right in front of my nose would make it disappear.

I moved in to a two-bedroom apartment. The boys shared one room and my daughter and I shared the other. The rent was cheap, and it was close to the kids' school. Against my better judgment, I agreed to give Brad a key. At first, he maintained boundaries using the key only to help me hang up pictures while I was at work. But very quickly, he started entering the apartment without my knowledge and searched my computer for clues to see if I was cheating on him. He was even checking my bedding for stains. To keep the drama to a minimum, I found myself in bed with Brad many times. I held a deep sense of obligation to continue satisfying him despite my commitment to Shane. Guilt and shame flowed freely through my heart every time I was with him. I told Shane when Brad and I were together as if the honesty would somehow breed forgiveness. Though I was not oblivious to the fact that it hurt him every time I confessed.

By Thanksgiving of that year, I was struggling to balance my new life. It became apparent that Shane was lying to me and hiding something. He would disappear when we had plans and not answer my calls. He would often get irritated with me when I wanted sex. He would guard his phone and make up grand stories about where he had been. I was losing control and began questioning my every move. When I stayed at his place, he would get text messages late in the night. Often, he was sleeping, and I could have easily looked at them. But something kept me from doing so. He would tell me that it was his friends' little sister who was drunk and not to worry. But the voice inside my head told me differently. I simply refused to listen. Instead of looking at the phone to see the messages that could easily shatter my tender heart, I would quietly leave and go back to my apartment without even a goodbye.

On one of the nights when Shane disappeared, I invited an old friend to come over and hang out. I had no intentions of it turning sexual but quickly discovered that he did. My initial instinct was to give in to his advances, after all, I suspected that Shane was being unfaithful. But as my friend began to kiss me and moved his hands toward my breasts, all I could think of was Shane. It was something I had never experienced before. I didn't know I had the capacity to fight off the cravings. I pushed him away and made him leave. I was determined to stop being that girl. I refused to let the addiction direct me any longer. Shane was the only person I wanted now, and I wasn't about to let anything pull me away from him. So, I continued to ignore my gut and focused on how to save our relationship.

Just before Christmas, the doctor discovered a lump in my breast. They scheduled surgery to have it removed the day before Shane was scheduled to leave for Texas. He told me he was going to see his parents, though, his story left me cynical. I asked him to stay with me the night of my procedure, but he held his ground and refused, citing a need for sleep before he left to the airport early the next day. His rejection shattered me, and my heart began to harden once again. It would have been easy enough to go home to Brad but there was no solace in that. Instead, I lay awake in my bed, riddled with pain from the surgery and the pain of rejection from Shane. I soaked my pillow in tears that night, believing that I was destined to live life lost and alone. While he was gone, Shane only called me twice and if I tried to call him, he wouldn't answer. I fought back the thoughts of a truth I knew to be real and settled on the idea that I would do whatever it took to never lose Shane Andrews.

When I picked him up from the airport, he provided

me a quick peck on the lips. It was clear that he had been drinking when he opened his Facebook Messenger and began reading a message he had received from Brad. I couldn't tell if he was angry or hurt but he read the letter with a clear air of amusement as I drove. Brad wasn't telling him anything he didn't already know. I brushed it off, anxious to get back to his place so we could relax. My desire for him was incredible but he rejected every attempt I made at seducing him. When I left him that night, I was confused by his rejection and consumed by the fate that seemed inevitable. I did my best to shrug off the overwhelming sense of dread and a few days later, when Brad came over to pick up the kids, I experienced a wave of clarity. We were arguing and began pushing one another. The reality hit me, only I had the capacity to change this situation. Something in my mind clicked and I realized that it was time to file for divorce. I hired an attorney that day. The moment I told him; Shane became Shane again.

Not long after Christmas, my gut feelings were confirmed when a message was left for Shane at the office by a woman named Jenna. It was crazy of me to take the message and return the call myself. But desperation can sometimes breed insanity. When she answered the phone, I asked her if she was Shane's girlfriend. She confirmed that she was, and I responded by letting her know that I was as well. She told me about the time they spent together; every heart wrenching detail. I could feel the blood drain from my face as she spoke. They had plans to get married and start a family. He had promised her that he was going to move to Texas to be with her and even spent time looking for work while he was there. The extent of his betrayal was staggering. By the time our conversation ended, I was numb and in an altered state of mind. I called Shane to my office and gave him one chance to come clean about her. He didn't. Only after I explained the phone conversation I had earlier that morning did he admit to what he had done.

We had betrayed one another in the worst way. But it was clear that we both held a desire for one another, so deep and so strong, that we would be able to overcome the demons between us. We talked about our infidelity long in to that night. He held me while I cried for the trust that had been broken. And somehow, I was able to conclude that our darkened souls could find their way back. A big part of me believed that I deserved the pain Shane inflicted on me. After all, look at what I had done to Brad. An even bigger part of me knew that despite the lies between us, it was not a coincidence that Shane and I were brought together. We agreed to continue with our relationship and to make valiant effort at putting the past behind us. It was not going to be an easy feat, but one I was anxiously willing to conquer.

As we moved forward, Shane allowed the best parts of himself to be revealed. Our love continued to grow and slowly we became stronger. The kids loved him and were happy when he was around. Things were going well, and the divorce was almost final. The kids and Shane had become my main focus so it's easy to look back and understand how I began to lose the company I had worked so hard to build for my dad. I was distracted by my new life and that gave my brother and Val the perfect opportunity to exploit me in my time of weakness.

As the divorce date approached, I was leaning heavily on my brother to assist me with my duties. By that time, it was known that Shane and I were together. Though not happy about it, my parents chose not to fight it and seemed to accept Shane as the new man in my life. My brother was supportive and patiently assisted me as I worked to get things back on track. Everything seemed to be coming together well. I was experiencing happiness for the first time in years. It appeared as though the real fairy tale I had dreamt of when I was a little girl was finally coming true.

Within a few months after the divorce, we bought a house close to the shop. It was far from the kids' school so there was a lot of driving involved. But everyone loved the house and we were all determined to make it work. I had it all. My dad, the kids, Shane, and a good career. My need for the high had completely disappeared and my ability to hope for the future had returned. I believed that I had finally found the antidote to my addiction. I was in a constant state of joy, blissfully unaware of the turmoil brewing around me.

CHAPTER 19
22 DAYS

Trauma comes in many forms. My whole life I had thought that PTSD was earmarked for soldiers. I thought I had no right to consider situations in my life as traumatic. I was comparing trauma for trauma and it seemed unfair of me to think that I could consider the events in my life as tragic as those of a soldier. Christina taught me to accept my trauma for what it was and helped me to understand that everyone's brain works differently. As we moved through our sessions, the instances of trauma seemed to add up. For whatever reason, my brain couldn't handle things in a way that would prevent damage.

****

Life was moving along well. We were moved in to the new house and everyone was settling in nicely. The extra driving wasn't ideal, but I felt it was worth it for us to have a home that we all loved and felt comfortable in. Our first Christmas in the new house was coming up and I was excited to have two trees and tons of rooms to decorate. The weekend after Thanksgiving, Shane and the boys put up lights on the outside and we watched Christmas movies when they were done. We were cheerful despite the chest colds we all seemed to be contracting. After a few days of illness, we learned that we all had strep throat. The antibiotics helped the kids and I get back to normal life quickly. Shane, however, wasn't getting any better. He had been working long hours to impress my dad and prove his loyalty to me and my family. He was run down and suffering exhaustion even before he got sick. He was rapidly going downhill and refused to go to the doctor.

December 01, 2010 began like any other day for me. Shane was laid up by the illness, but I needed to get the kids to school and get myself to work. I made sure he was set up with everything he would need and told him that I would come home for lunch to check on him. It was shortly after I arrived at work when I got the phone call from Shane. He was coughing up blood and felt weak. He needed to go to the doctor but didn't think he could drive himself. As I was on my way home, he joked with me that he wasn't going to die and assured me that I didn't need to worry. By the time we got to the doctor's office, he had filled half an empty water bottle with the blood he was spitting up. The x-rays were read as "unfounded" and the doctor urged me to take Shane to the emergency room. Upon our arrival at the hospital, things moved along quickly. They got him hooked up to IV saline and antibiotics. It didn't take long for them to decide that they would admit him. The kids were scheduled to be with Brad that night, so I stayed at the hospital with him until visiting hours were over. We snuggled on his bed and watched television. Before I left, he once again assured me that he was going to be okay and told me not to worry. I called to check on him before I went to bed and he was doing well.

When I arrived at the hospital the next morning, they

had moved him to another floor. He was quarantined and in worse shape than I left him. There were doctors and nurses moving in and out of his room in a panicked state. They threw a face mask at me and told me I could have a few minutes with him before they moved him to the ICU. I was confused and scared as I approached him. Shane was out of sorts and began mumbling instructions to me about who to notify if he died. When I began to cry, he scolded me and told me that I needed to be strong for him so he could be weak. It was a pivotal moment for me when I realized that I could be strong for someone else. After only a few minutes, the nurse told me that I needed to go while they prepped him to be moved to ICU. She told me that a doctor would come speak to me shortly and showed me to the waiting room. The first call I made was to my dad. I was scared and didn't know what to do. I began to cry as I explained to him what was going on. He got angry at me, started yelling, and told me to call him back when I was calm. I stared at the phone in my hand after he hung up wondering how I was going to calm down. It hit me like a ton of bricks. After all the years of trying to win my dad's love and acceptance, I clearly hadn't won his support. The next call I made was to Brad. I explained the situation and he agreed to keep the kids for as long as I needed him to. We both acknowledged that they were too young to see Shane like this. It was the only civil conversation he and I had mustered since the divorce.

After what seemed like hours but was plausibly only a few minutes, the doctor found me in the waiting room and explained the next steps. Shane was very sick, but they did not know with what. They were moving him to the Intensive Care Unit and were going to do a biopsy of his lungs to help determine the cause of his illness. He assured me that they would get to the bottom of it and asked me if there was anyone I could call to come keep me company. My mind went blank.

I was trapped in a nightmare and couldn't wake up. My body went numb and I stared at my phone, unsure of who I could call. Without conscious thought, I called Shane's brother, Tanner, and told him he needed to come down quickly. It wasn't his company that I wanted as much as it was that I knew Shane needed his brother.

The nurses captured my attention as they were pushing Shane to ICU and told me I needed to come along. He was awake and seemingly more aware of what was going on. He was making jokes and trying to ease my mind as we rode up to the fourth floor on the back elevator. I did my best to maintain my composure and be strong for him as we entered the ICU. The many rooms formed a square around the circular nurse's station. Shane's room was immediately to the left as you entered that wing of the floor. The sign above the door said "4th Floor North ICU". The entrance to his room was set with two glass windows and a glass door. The room was small and had a long, narrow window toward the top of the back wall. There was much commotion as the nurses moved around to get him set up and hooked up to all the monitors. As they started a second IV, Shane continued to try and joke with me and held my hand tighter than he ever had. Two doctors arrived very shortly after he was settled and told me that I could stand outside the room while they performed the procedure. It didn't dawn on me how serious the situation was, even then. My mind was foggy as I watched through the window. When they started to put the tube down his throat for the biopsy, I turned my head. My stomach never could handle watching any type of medical procedures. I froze when I heard the words "Code Blue" come over the loud speaker. Doctors and nurses began running past me, moving in and out of Shane's room at what seemed like lightning speed. I stood, frozen, unable to move. Yet, somehow, I found the courage to turn my head back toward the window. There were so many people in the room and so many machines. They worked together like clockwork as they performed CPR and provided each other with instructions. Though I heard nothing they were saying. Only the words "Code Blue" and "Clear" echoed in my head. I stared in disbelief as they worked tirelessly to save his life.

The female doctor made eye contact with me from inside the room and, as if realizing for the first time that I was there, promptly came to my side and asked me to walk with her. We exited the ICU and walked toward the long hallway that lead to the waiting room. The entire south side of the walkway was lined with large windows. It was cold and overcast outside. She stopped when we were halfway down the hall and placed her hand on my shoulder. "Shane is very sick." She started. "We are waiting for the ventilator so we can intubate him." She went on to explain that they were unable to get the biopsy because he crashed, and they would need him to get a little better before they would consider that procedure again. They were placing him in a medically induced coma in hopes that he could heal. I began to cry uncontrollably but managed to ask her if he was going to die. She merely responded, "Shane is very sick, but we will do everything we can to help him." I grabbed the railing and my body fell against the window. She stood next to me, holding my arm to ensure that I didn't fall completely to the floor. I heard Tanner's voice and looked up to see him walking quickly toward us and I think he was asking me what was wrong. I looked to the doctor and asked her to please tell him. I couldn't bear the thought of repeating her words. It seemed like we stood there for hours staring at each other before walking to a table in the waiting room to sit down.

At some point, Shannon showed up. I'm not sure if I called her or if Tanner did. I simply looked up and there she was. When the nurse finally came back to tell Tanner and I that we could go see him, the sun was setting. As we walked back through the long hallway, the nurse did her best to prepare us for what we would see when we entered his room. She informed us that Shane did not take well to the normal ventilator and that they had no choice but to get the oscillating ventilator from the NICU and that is what took so long. She explained the difference, though, I was hardly listening. When I turned the corner to enter his room, the words "code blue" echoed in my head and visions of people running toward him ran through my mind. I closed my eyes, squirted the hand sanitizer on my hands, and pulled my face mask back up. Shane was still on quarantine because they did not know what was wrong with him. When I opened my eyes and looked inside his room, I was brought to tears once again.

He looked so small in the bed. The ventilator was loud and frightening. There were IV's on both sides of his arms and the room was dark. The nurse continued to talk to us about Shane's condition and give us instructions, though, I didn't hear a word she said. I merely sat next to him and lay my head on his arm. I couldn't imagine my life without him; I had just found him. A different doctor came in to speak with us. He advised that Shane was suffering from Acute Respiratory Distress Syndrome, but they weren't sure what the cause of it was. They were calling in an Infectious Disease Doctor from the east coast to evaluate his case. We were asked to continue wearing the face masks until they had more answers. The doctor did not know if he would survive and asked us to prepare for the worst. My heart bled and my body began to tremble. After an hour or so, Tanner convinced me to go sit with him in the waiting room so we could make some calls.

Shannon was still sitting at the table and her daughter had brought us dinner. I wasn't hungry, but she somehow convinced me to eat. Tanner called his Mom and Shannon encouraged me to call my dad. He was already in a foul mood when he answered the phone. I explained the situation to him, and he started to lecture me about how this is why I shouldn't be dating an employee. He needed me at work and now he was short three employees; me, Shane, and Tanner. As if it was somehow my fault that Shane was in a hospital bed dying. He continued to lecture me, and I stared at Shannon as tears began to fill my eyes. Anger promptly took over and I hung up on him. I had never hung up on or even considered hanging up on my dad before. His lack of empathy and understanding wasn't what I needed in that moment. I immediately called my brother. He exhibited great empathy and concern as I explained the situation. When I told him how Dad had reacted, he got angry and told me that he would take care of it for me. It was one of the few times that my brother was ever there for me; and it was the last.

The rest of the night was spent sitting in the waiting room and sitting with Shane. Shannon and Tanner stayed with me the whole night and none of us slept. I didn't want to leave Shane's side. I believed that he could hear me and that if he knew I was there, maybe he would find the strength to survive. I think I read that in a book or something. But as morning came, the doctor advised me that he was getting worse. He needed a blood transfusion and plasma transfusions. They were going to start a central line in his upper arm. By the end of the day, there were multiple IV Poles behind the head of his bead and numerous bags of various fluids hanging from them. It was like nothing I had ever seen before; not even in the movies. They were having difficulty regulating his temperature and were having problems with the oscillating ventilator. I was helpless and began to lose my new-found hope. The scarier the news got, the more I stayed by his side. There had to be something I could do.

In the days that followed, Shannon never left my side. Though I hadn't slept and was exhausted, I refused to leave the hospital. His temperature wouldn't go down, but I was able to figure out that he was simply hot. I asked the nurse to strip him down naked and bring a fan in to the room. She was reluctant at first, but willing to try anything. She did as I asked, using only a small towel to cover his man parts. Within an hour, his temperature was in normal limits. That seemed to open the nurse's hearts and they all became friendly with me. It's as if my connection to Shane's needs made them trust me and we quickly formed a bond. The oscillating ventilator was loud and annoyed most everyone who came in the room. But even the technicians couldn't figure out how to fix it and the only other one the hospital had was broken. Because Shane was such a big man, they were having difficulty moving him from side to side; something they needed to do so his lungs could heal. They brought in an air-ride bed that tilted the way they needed so they no longer had to physically move him. The bond I had with the nurses meant that they allowed me to stay with Shane during all hours, regardless of quiet times. Honestly, it gave the nurses a bit of break from the noise as well. He was set for twenty four-hour, one-on-one care so they weren't supposed to leave his room. They set up their mobile station right outside his door and I quickly became an expert at reading the numbers on the screens so I could get their attention if needed. I was also the only one who wasn't bothered by the noise of the ventilator. I don't know if I ever really heard the noise; it was nothing to me. All that mattered was making sure that Shane knew I was there.

After a few days, the nurse told Shane's Mom to come and say her goodbyes. She lived in another State and had been calling frequently to check on him. Additionally, she was his next of kin, since he and I were not married, so decisions were being run through her via telephone. Within a couple days of her arrival, she released decision making rights to me and suddenly, Shane's life was in my hands. I agreed to let his mom have a Catholic Priest come and pray over him. Or maybe he was reading him his last rights; I honestly didn't know. I hadn't been involved in that religion for years and was merely grasping at straws. Anything that might help heal him and bring him back to me was worth trying.

By the beginning of his second week in ICU, I had not slept or left the hospital. Shannon convinced me to let her take me to her house so I could, at minimum, take a nap. I vaguely remember taking a shower and sleeping on her bed for a half hour or so. I had no desire to be away from Shane. As if being next to him would ensure that he would survive. His condition wasn't changing and nothing the doctors did was working. They continued to prepare me for the worst and Shannon convinced me to go to the hospital chapel with her and pray. I hadn't spoken to God since I was a young child. I felt out of place and uncomfortable. But again, I was willing to try anything.

By the end of the second week, it was time for me to face reality and start returning to my life. My dad was still highly irritated at my absence and Tanner had returned to work earlier in the week. That Friday, I found the strength to go home, shower, and attempt a nap. I allowed myself only to sleep for twenty minutes that day. There was nothing I could do that would allow my mind to rest knowing that Shane was going to die. I was sad and heartbroken as I looked around our bedroom. I lay on his side of the bed so that I could smell him. After my short nap, I got up to dress and head back to the hospital. As I put my shirt on, I began to cry uncontrollably. Without thinking, I dropped to my knees, crying and screaming; begging God to save him. A God I had never known, but one I needed to believe in at that moment. After about five minutes of crying and screaming to God, I felt foolish and stood to wipe my tears. But when I got in my car and began my trek back to the hospital, I felt an overwhelming sense of peace come over my body. I somehow knew that everything was going to be okay.

Upon my arrival at the hospital, his condition hadn't changed. Shannon and all our new friends were right where I had left them in the waiting room. I approached Shane's bed with a different feeling that day. I smiled when I saw him and kissed his forehead. I whispered to him that everything was going to be okay. I stayed with him throughout the night and for most of the weekend. I told him that I needed to return to work and promised him that I would come see him every day. I asked him not to die without me there. It was a strange, one sided, conversation. One I felt oddly at peace having.

I returned to work the third week and did my best to avoid my dad at all cost. Though I'm sure I didn't get much done. I would leave early in the day so I could spend a few hours with Shane before picking up the kids. He still wasn't getting better. None of the doctors, not even the Infectious Disease Doc could figure out why he wasn't healing. Shane had a note in his chart that he was allergic to penicillin, although, his mother didn't know why. One night, mid-week of the third week, they asked me if I would give them permission to administer the penicillin, knowing that he might not be able to survive an allergic reaction. I never considered any possibilities and as if someone else was speaking for me, I quickly said yes. That Saturday, I found myself sitting next to Shane wondering if he would ever come back to me. I glanced out the door and noticed his doctors and the nurse gathered around the x-ray they had taken earlier in the morning. I looked away as the nurse walked toward me, unsure if I had strength left to hear the words I was certain she was going to say. But instead, her voice was filled with happiness and when I turned, she smiled at me and advised that they were ordering the regular ventilator be brought up immediately. Shane's lungs were healing, and the oscillating ventilator was giving him too much air. It was a miracle, even the doctors said so. He was going to survive, words no one had dared speak during the sixteen days he had already been there. Within days, Shane was awake. They sent him home a few days later. Twenty-two days of pure fear and there he was, home in time for Christmas. Though I did not practice any type of faith at the time, I knew, for sure, that God brought him back to me and that Shane Andrews was meant to be in my life forever.

CHAPTER 20
THE CRAZY MAKERS

*"They call them the crazy makers." Christina had an amused
smile on her face as she watched my reaction. You know, those
people that tell you what you said isn't really what you said and
then tell you what you did isn't really what you did and then
tell you what you remember isn't really what you remember?
Yes, those are the crazy makers. After a while, you begin to
think that you're the crazy one.*

****

As Shane began the long process of healing at home, I was
able to put my mind back in to work. I made silent amends
with my dad, but the dynamics and logistics of the business
began to change. My brother and I seemed to have some sort
of bond as a result of his support while Shane was in the ICU.
But without realizing it, I had given him the inlet he needed to
take over my company. Or, rather, dismantle it. The first thing
to go was Dispatch. My brother convinced my dad and I that

it was best to consolidate the dispatch centers and all my dispatchers were let go. I began traveling between shops multiple times a day. My brother and I started sharing the on-call position in a rotating fashion. I would help him supervise his employee's while he was busy with association duties. On the surface, we seemed to be working in perfect harmony. But in the background, Val was complaining about me to anyone that would listen and constantly accused me of not doing my job. Over time, my happiness turned to extreme stress and it started to take a toll. But I was better able to manage it with Shane by my side. Still determined to prove something to my dad, I pushed on.

Though we had our scuffle while Shane was in the hospital, Dad and I seemed to be building a stronger relationship than I ever expected. He called me every morning at the same time; if he didn't call, I would call him and make sure he was okay. I came to rely on his morning calls almost as if it provided the comfort and validation. I needed to know that he loved me. He came over to our house and helped us if we needed it. Even my brother came over once and helped us put in a new water heater. I was finally part of the family; a family I had spent thirty-three years vying to belong to. I wasn't going to let a bit of stress get in the way of that. But as the pattern goes, that's when everything started to change.

My brother and I were trying to work closely together within the business and the association. I relied on him and he relied on me. Val did not like that. She began to amp up her constant scrutiny of me and bitched to my parents about me the way Grandma used to bitch when I was nine years old. And, just like when I was nine years old, my parents believed her and not me. Every day became a battle. One I wasn't interested in fighting. It upset Dad when I argued with him about it so I chose to work harder and did everything I could to stay off her radar. But there was nothing I could do to stay off her radar. I had always been her target and still didn't know why.

To add insult to injury, I began having problems with board members from the association. After four years, my coordination of the show was no longer to their liking. When I asked my brother for help, since he was the President, he sat back and did nothing. My dad in fact had witnessed some of the treatment I received and did nothing at the advice of my brother. At the end of the fifth-year show, and with a very heavy heart, I resigned as the Show Coordinator. I felt like I had let Walter down. I broke my promise and I let our dreams for the show disappear in one moment. But maybe I hadn't broken my promise. I knew resigning was what I needed to do for the sake of happiness. The stress emulating from Val was more than enough to occupy my mind. I couldn't continue if the show was going to add more weight on my shoulders than I already had. After submitting my resignation, a chain of events began that drove me down a path I wasn't expecting to travel.

It was a warm summer night when I got the call sometime around one am. One of our drivers had been struck and killed on the side of the road. Something we in the towing industry were all too familiar with. It was the very reason that it was commonplace for me to be headed off to a funeral in a tow truck. I woke Shane and told him the news. We sat silently in the dark, both of us in shock. After a while, I ran to the bathroom and that's when my phone rang again. Shane answered it but the caller did not want to wait. It was my dad. When I called him back, he began yelling at me for not answering the phone. I tried to explain but he wouldn't listen, he only went on to yell at me for calling people and telling them what had happened. I was confused and asked what he meant. He advised, still yelling at me, that Shannon had texted my brother about the accident. He assumed I was the one who told her. At some point he hung up on me. I turned to Shane, stunned and a bit irritated by the interaction. I hadn't contacted anyone and had no intention of doing so, that's not the type of person I am. I found out later that it was one of Shannon's drivers who heard the call on the police scanner and immediately notified her of the situation. She was simply reaching out to my brother to offer her support. Dad never apologized to me for the accusation. That night was the first time I experienced clarity about why I was working for the family business. The puzzle pieces were coming together, and I began to reconsider my definition of happiness.

But that was not the time to worry about me and my problems. It was time to care for the driver's family and the literal mountain of paperwork that comes when such a tragedy strikes your business. The following weeks were filled with media, insurance companies, the family of the fallen, and helping the other employees cope. It was exhausting and time consuming. Thankfully, we were all too busy for bickering.

When the dust finally settled, the holidays were approaching. Val began her incessant complaining again, only this time, she made it personal. She cried that I was writing my blog about her and saying mean things about her on Facebook. Dad ordered me to stop posting and told me that I needed to stop writing my blog. She began making disparaging comments about me and Shane to employees. Boundaries were crossed and once again, I began to find clarity. A voice whispered in my ear, telling me that this was not the path to happiness. By the beginning of 2012, I lived in a silent state of uncertainty. My company had all but had its name changed and I spent most of my time at my brothers shop. I continued working tirelessly, hoping that it would somehow make my dad believe in me enough to see the truth about what Val was doing. But it made no impact. He maintained his expectation that I would somehow make her stop. By spring, I found myself crying daily and was consumed with trying to figure out how to stop her. Then another bomb dropped.

My brother called me early in the morning on a Monday to let me know that the son of a competitor, Miles, had committed suicide over the weekend. My head started to spin, and my brothers voice became faint in my ear. I was light years away from conscious thought at that moment. My stomach flipped and my chest tightened. We had just spoken to Miles that weekend. He had invited Shane and I to the races. He was a good man, young, with a lot to learn, but kind hearted and eager. He too was working to take over his family business someday. We had so many things in common, yet, we didn't really know each other that well. I sat in silence for hours that morning. Wondering why and eventually concluding that his pain was simply too much to bare. I went about my day somber and out of sorts.

Later that week, as we coordinated yet another tow truck procession in honor of our fallen brother, I met my mother for dinner. I sat and listened as she preached to me how selfish Miles was for leaving his family that way. She called him a coward and explained how such an act was unforgivable. I stared at her as if she was a stranger. I wondered to myself who exactly had raised me because I was certain it wasn't her. I tried to change the subject, but it ended up on Val and that was not the subject I was going for. Though, she did listen to my concerns and offered empathy for my situation. She concluded that I should start keeping a written record of everything I did at work each day so that when Val complained to Dad, I could show him my log. It sounded ludicrous to me, but I was certain that Mom had put a lot of thought in to it and had deduced that this was the only way. So, I agreed.

The following day, I attempted to talk to Dad about my concerns with Val. I told him that I was tired of the fight and that I was one foot out the door. He said he understood where I was coming from, but the look on his face told me he didn't have the strength to deal with it. I was asking him to make a choice between me or my brother. I didn't verbalize that, but it was what I was doing because dealing with Val meant friction between him and my brother. Without knowing it, Dad made a choice that day and I had an epiphany. All the years I spent trying to prove myself worthy of his love were in vain. No matter what I did, it wasn't going to be enough and Dad would never believe me or believe in me the way he did my brother. Dad would never love me the way I needed him to love me. It was a moment of clarity that damn near knocked me off my feet. Suddenly, I was four years old again and my dad was wrestling with me on the floor. That's what I had been looking for all these years. Unsure of what to do next, I proceeded to live as I had been living. Waking every morning wondering what lies I would need to oppose that day. After Miles' funeral, the answers became clear.

It was the straw that broke the camel's back. We had a dispatcher who had a flare for the dramatic. His name was Shawn. He lied to my brother one evening and told him that I was screaming at him over the phone. I tried to explain the reality of the situation to my brother, but he cut me off and said he had reviewed the video. The video that had no audio. He told me that given the nature of Shawn's body language, he believed that I was lying, and that Shawn was telling the truth. Frustrated and desperate for someone to believe in me, I called my mother and explained the situation to her. My dad was in the background and got angry that I called her and not him. Either way, it was irrelevant. Neither my brother nor my dad believed me. That's when it became clear to me; how to save that little girl. It was time for me to leave.

I called Nora first and asked her if her company had any job openings. As luck would have it, they did. Shane and I knew that he couldn't possibly continue working there without me. He would only become the next target. The cut in pay I was going to take was devastating and that meant that Shane would have to pick up the slack. But true to his nature, Shane supported my decision and vowed to care for our family no matter what it took. There was no judgment and no second guessing. He believed in me and believed me when I told him the truth about what was happening. For the first time in my life, I was looking love straight in the eyes.

I knew that if I tried to give notice, my dad, my brother, or my mom would convince me to stay. Unfortunately, that meant I had to walk away quietly without notice. I also knew that I would lose my family. I figured that out when I walked away so many years ago. Only this time, I would be losing a bigger family. My industry family. My children would lose their grandparents and their uncle. It would be a painful break, but I knew it was a break that needed to happen for sanity's sake. The crazy makers were taking over, and I wasn't interested in losing my new found hope because of them.

April 12, 2012, I left my brother a note and made a copy of it for my mother. I knew he would lie to them and tell them I left nothing. Which is exactly what he did. I had planned it well, all the way down to getting my own phone with a new number. Only my sister had my contact information. She was never a factor in my decision. I knew that she would be there, no matter what. She was my one true constant, my only confidant.

When I pulled up to my new job that morning, I found myself pondering what was happening at the family business. I wondered if my brother or my mom had found the note yet. I was curious if my employees knew. Leaving them was likely the hardest part of walking away. Yet, I knew this was the step I needed to take if I ever wanted to find peace in my life. I couldn't be family owned and operated any longer. So, I stepped out of my car, looked around my new surroundings and realized; I was, once again, that brave little girl.

EPILOGUE

It's been seven years since I left the family business. I have only seen my dad once in that time. The need for his love and acceptance has dissipated. My mother and I see each other a few times a year but I keep her at an arm's length. Forgiveness has not come easily and is a difficult piece in my recovery. But I no longer desire their validation.

Being brave doesn't always come easily. I've struggled with jobs, depression, and friendships since the day I left. I see Christina on a monthly basis, and she continues to guide me through my recovery. But I have something to hold on to now, the one thing that was missing from my life for so many years; hope.

I began attending a Christian church in 2015. I never thought I would become a woman of faith after the life I lived. But it has helped me a great deal on my quest to find happiness and peace. Once I was able to get past the live band and Pastor Jim in his tee-shirt and jeans, I was able to open my heart to Jesus and my mind to the possibility of healing. Almost immediately, I began to attend the church's recovery program and enrolled in a 12 Step Study. I signed up to volunteer and encouraged my children to try out the student ministries. Slowly, I started to unpack the wounds of my youth which unfortunately, caused my depression to spike. That's what led me to Christina. When I walked in to her to office, unsure and untrusting, I couldn't have imagined the journey I was about to take. I believe that if it hadn't been for church and Christina, I may never have found my way.

My sister continues to be my one constant and I have made many new friends over the years. I finally feel that sense of belonging that I spent most of my life looking for.

Shane and I are happily married, and my cravings have never resurfaced. He has walked this journey by my side and has believed in me every difficult step of the way. My children are growing quickly and occupy most of our time. There is an overall sense of peace in my life now. The road to recovery is hard. But it's definitely worth the trek.

ABOUT THE AUTHOR

I am a forty-two-year-old mother of three and a full time Author. *Brave Little Girl* is my first book. It took me nineteen months to complete this book and was one of the toughest journey's I have ever taken.

My goal is to empower people around the world who suffer from PTSD, Depression, Anxiety, or any other ailment as a result of their past. I believe that every person deserves the opportunity to heal without judgement or ridicule. It is my goal to give readers hope based off of my experiences of pain.

Learn more at: http://www.emersynkane.com

Made in the USA
Middletown, DE
04 May 2019